Deadly Secrets Hunters Reign

The Crown Series Book 1

E. Bowser

Copyright © 2019 by E. Bowser

All rights reserved

The Deadly Secrets Series is a work of fiction. Names, characters, businesses, places, events, and incidents are either the products of the author's imagination or used in a fictitious manner. Any resemblance to actual persons, living or dead, or actual events is purely coincidental.

Acknowledgments

I want to thank God for letting me be able to write the stories that I love. I also want to thank my mother and the love of my life for putting up with me. I want to thank my friends who keep pushing and believing in me. Big thank you to Sinful Secrets with a Deadly Bite Group. All of you have supported me through this series. Thank you to everyone that reads the series that contacts me on Facebook, Twitter, and IG. I always love to hear from you. That is what keeps me writing.

GIO VAUGHN

Red - Pure Blood
Blue - Blue Blood
Gold - Other

Contents

1. Prologue — 1
2. Chapter One — 6
3. Chapter Two — 14
4. Chapter Three — 23
5. Chapter Four — 31
6. Chapter Five — 39
7. Chapter Six — 48
8. Chapter Seven — 56
9. Chapter Eight — 66
10. Chapter Nine — 73
11. Chapter Ten — 84
12. Chapter Eleven — 93
13. Chapter Twelve — 102
14. Chapter Thirteen — 112

15.	Chapter Fourteen	121
16.	Chapter Fifteen	131
17.	Chapter Sixteen	138
18.	Chapter Seventeen	147
19.	Chapter Eighteen	157
20.	Chapter Nineteen	166
21.	Chapter Twenty	175
22.	Chapter Twenty-One	186
23.	Chapter Twenty-Two	196
24.	Chapter Twenty-Three	205
25.	Chapter Twenty-Four	213
26.	Epilogue	220
27.	The End until next time...	227
About Author		228
Also By The Author		231

Prologue

JESSIAH VAUGHN

Sometime in the past

I held Kayla close to my heart as I moved through the trees. I knew I should have taken her home long ago, where I knew she would be protected. I didn't know what my parents would do if they found out their first-born heir to the throne, and the one that everyone thought would gain Gio's power, was willing to give it all up. "We're almost there, my Kindred." I could feel her push her face into my neck as her hot tears burned my skin. It was funny because I knew I wouldn't be the one, but the child my mother was carrying was the one to sit on the throne and who would save this world. He would wield the power that I think no one else, including me, should have. I knew it wouldn't be Damon, but I couldn't see why the gifts skipped him. When my little brother was born, the world cried. The animals fled, and the sky cried for us all because he would be the fall of our family. It was already destined to be that way. I hated the knowledge that came to me when it wanted to. That was one curse of our bloodline. The incompletion of the visions was a horrible thing to give any being.

"Jessiah, the baby is coming. We will not make it much further." Kayla said, wincing at the pain. I knew she was right, but we had to stay ahead of those damned Necromancers.

Before I met Kayla, my life had been to find my father's mother, Selena Vaughn. I found where I thought my Grandmother Selena may have fallen during the battle to close the old gates so it would not escape to this Earth. When I reached the island that shouldn't have been there, that's when I saw her. She stood there, a tall, beautiful woman with long dark silken hair that fell over smooth mahogany skin. She stared back at me. She stood at the edge where the seawater met the sand. Her clothes were made from the island's plants, but her weapons were unlike anything I had ever seen. She held two long poles with sharpened ends. I thought they were just spears, but I could tell they weren't anything from this world as I got closer.

"You finally made it." Her voice was soft and light, almost as if it were music. It took me a full minute to reply because she spoke another language, but I could fully understand it. I had no idea how that would even be possible.

"Who are you?" She looked away to the side at the storm brewing in the distance.

"No time for that. Let's move." She pivoted and ran into the jungles. If I didn't know any better, she had to be a human, but what human could move that fast? I followed her into the jungle, and it forever changed my life.

I shook my head to clear that memory away. That was so long ago I had no idea what she was then, but I knew now, and I had to protect her and our baby. It turned out I wasn't the one she was looking for, but she was what my heart was looking for. She was mine, and she turned out to be my Kindred Soul, and she called me her other spirit.

"We can rest here," I said as I placed her on the ground.

"Your child will not wait much longer." She smiled as she held her belly. We are close to my family. They will protect you.

"Do they even know that you are alive?" She asked, searching for my eyes. They knew it would take me a while to find anything about my grandmother, so I know they couldn't have lost hope.

"Yes, but I know they don't expect you to return with a pregnant woman." She smiled weakly.

"Probably not, but they won't believe that that pregnant woman who is self-fallen to help this world picked me to love."

"That wasn't my plan, but then I met you." She looked into my eyes, and I saw their pain before she screamed. I heard the roar off in the distance, and I knew they were getting close.

"Kayla, we have to move," I said, lifting her in my arms once more.

"I'm sorry, Jessiah. Your daughter is a handful already." I smiled at the thought of my child. Everyone would be safe if I could make it home with Kayla and the book.

"Jessiah, you know if I do not make it through this childbirth, you must find Cross. He is the only one who can understand this text." The small bronze book that was clutched in her hands glowed with a light not of the world.

"You will be able to give it to him yourself," I growled. I could see a few small houses up ahead. I knew we were close to my family's land. The wolves who lived on this land were loyal, and I knew they would help. I sped up faster, knocking on the first door I came to. An older woman shifter answered the door.

"My Lord. What is the problem?" She looked us over and behind, trying to figure out where we came from.

"You are part of the Butler pack, correct?" I asked while moving quickly, passed her, and over to a bed in the corner.

"Yes, yes, now lay her down right here." The howls and screams were getting louder, and I had to do something to keep them safe.

"Where are your male shifters? Where is your Alpha?" I asked as I tried reaching out to my father but failed.

"They are not here, child. Do you not know what is going on?" I looked out of the windows, barely understanding what she was saying. Kayla screamed again, and I went to her.

"I think I want to name her Rose. Maybe she will name her daughter after a flower as well." I tried to smile, but that fell flat when the howling and growling went silent.

"What is going on around here? I need to get to Micah Vaughn."

"There is a war among the species. It is just such a shame, but our males went to fight along with the vampires." I looked at both women and realized this village was probably nothing but women and children, and I led what was after us here.

"Take care of them. I will be back after I lure them away." I removed my pack and pulled out the book leading them to Selena. "Kayla, make sure this book stays safe until I come back. We will stop them before figuring out how to break the seals my grandmother may have died for. We will not let the sacrifice you made to fall go in vain."

"You better come back to me. I don't regret falling if it meant I had time with you." I leaned in to kiss her forehead as beads of sweat dripped down her face.

"Take care of our child," I whispered and left before I could change my mind. I ran back into the trees. I would never let Marco get ahold of Kayla or my child. I will not allow him to find Selena either. Whatever

I had to do would be done. I would die for my Kindred Soul and protect my family and everyone in this world.

Chapter One

TARIA

It wasn't long after Camron and Hayley left that Michael popped up in my office. The look of terror in his eyes had Toya and me burst out laughing.

"Will you two shut the hell up?" He whispered. His gold eyes blazed at me.

"Aww, poor Mike, scared of a little girl. His little princess Lily," Toya said, standing up.

"Whatever," Michael said, moving away from the door. I looked at Toya and knew it was almost time for her and Quinn to get moving, and I wouldn't say I liked it. I knew they had to travel for a bit so Quinn could see all of his shifters and get things on track. I just wasn't ready for Toya to go, and my God, babies. Michael sat in the chair before my desk, staring at me.

"Taria, everything will be fine, and we will be back before you know it. Quinn and I still have some things to sort out in New Orleans. I feel more comfortable going there now that I have had some type of training." Toya said, coming around the desk. I stood up, hating the fact she was leaving because the last damn time she did, her ass was kidnapped. I leaned over to hug her short ass, and I could feel that bond of the witch and hunter snap in place.

"I think before you go, we should go out. Check out Na'na at her club and just spend some time together." I said, pulling away.

"That is what the hell I'm talkin' about. Shit, we haven't been anywhere like that since—"

"Since Quinn almost ripped Steven's head off his shoulders," Michael said with a half-smile.

"Shut up, Mike! He was just a little touchy, that's all. If he had, it wouldn't have been no love lost." Toya said, shrugging her shoulders. I shook my head when I heard giggling and screaming, along with a jolt to my arm.

"What the hell was that?" I asked as we both turned to the door. Lily was screaming for her father in a high pitch tone.

"Just a spell, so if you need me, I can feel where you will be and open a portal to get there." I raised a brow as my door crashed open, and Michael shook his head at me.

"Daddy, you said you would be right back. Uncle Cam left long ago, and you still haven't returned. I finished Garrett's hair forever ago." Lily said with wide brown eyes. Her black curly hair fell all around her face as she smiled at Michael. I moved around the desk, quickly taking pity on him.

"Lily, you don't want to do Mommy's hair?" I asked, kissing her cheek.

"Yeah, Lily, what about Auntie Toya? You haven't done my hair either?" Lily looked between us both, then back to Michael.

"Daddy, I have to do you later. Mommy and Aunt Toya really need my help. They are going out, and I can't let them go out like this." I bit my lip hard as hell while Toya fell out laughing. Michael stood up and stood beside us with an enormous smile.

"You got that, Lily. I will let you do what you gotta do, princess." He leaned over and kissed her and me on the cheek before disappearing.

"Oh, he is going to owe me for this!" Toya said, trying to catch her breath.

"Lily, how did you know Toya, and I were going somewhere?" The sparkle in her eyes and the smiling grin made me believe she was way older than I knew she was.

"I know a lot of things, Mommy." I looked over at LaToya as her laughter died off.

"Oh, lawd Taria. Your children are way too much for me," she said as Lily's smile grew wider.

After removing all the bows from my hair, I tucked Lily into bed. I returned to my room to get dressed and have a night out with my bestie. Doing something normal felt so out of the ordinary that I had no idea what to put on. The doors opened as Toya came in, holding three different pairs of shoes.

"I already know what you should wear, so chill." I should have known she would be back on her shit.

"Thank you." She dropped her shoes and went over to my walk-in closet, looking over everything I had.

"Taria, have you thought about us going out and other people recognizing us? I mean, I know I am sexy as shit and all, but I don't like to be gawked at." She said, pulling out a pair of red leather pants and a see-through black shirt. "Do you have a red lace bra?"

"Yes, I do, and I was hoping we could just play it off. I mean, we could go to a supernatural night club. Hell, we should go to Na'na's club." I said as I pulled open a drawer and found my red lace bra.

"I think you should wear some red bottom heels," Toya said, smiling at me.

"Yeah, I think not. You know damn well I hate heels. Plus, I need a place for my blades, and my boots are perfect."

"Ok, ok, compromise. How about you wear those thigh-high boots? That has a heel, and it still gives you a place for your knives." She rolled her eyes.

"Done. Now, why do you have all of these shoes in here?" I asked as she laid the outfit on the bed.

"I didn't know which one to pick." She said, crossing her arms.

"What are you wearing?"

"How am I supposed to know that answer if I don't know what shoes I want to wear?" I raised my hands as the door opened again, and Michael stepped inside. "Michael, what shoes should I wear?" His eyebrow raised as he looked over the choices.

"The all-black shoes with the diamonds going up the heel. That one will give you more height and be deadly in a fight."

"I like the way you think." She picked up her shoes and rushed out of the room.

"Why do you indulge her?" I asked as he stalked over toward me. I already had my shirt off when he pulled me into him. He kissed my neck before his fangs sank in. "Fuck," I whispered. The heat between my legs grew as his cool hands caressed my skin. He pulled back, licking my neck.

"Because she is the little sister I never had. She's funny as fuck and doesn't even try, but I would never tell her that." I smiled as I pulled him down, trying to get a bite myself. "Naw, sweetheart. You need to go feed for real before you hit the club. I want to be your dessert when you get home."

"Ahh, shit, now we are talking. Maybe I should stay in tonight." I said, smiling.

"You both need this, but you will go to Sinful Secrets. No human club right now."

"I can go where I want to go," I said, raising both eyebrows.

"Right. You and LaToya are going to Sinful Secrets." I stared into his eyes as the gold grew molten. I wasn't going to question him on this one, but damn. I wanted to go somewhere normal.

"Fine."

"I know it's fine," he said, pulling away.

"And it will be Toya and me that are going. I refuse to take anyone else. I can handle myself."

"I think you should–"

"Michael!"

"Ok, fine," he growled. I knew he wasn't happy, but fuck that. We needed space and time before she left to do important shit for herself and Quinn. Hell, I needed this before life as a Queen really took over. His agreeing so quickly didn't bode well for some reason, and I knew someone would be following along.

"So since Na'na and Marcus are going to check out this mermaid situation, I think we should send Elaine back to NY. She has done a good job and should be with Kya. They have a lot of catching up to do." I said as I sat down in front of the vanity. I looked at myself in the mirror, and sometimes I couldn't believe the differences. My eyes were lighter, and I sometimes saw slight lightning flashes in them.

"Yeah, I still need to talk to Marcus about that. This will be interesting, but I think it would be a good idea for Elaine. I don't want her this close to Sarah. She is a part of the Van Allan bloodline, whether we like it or not. Some things have been brought to my attention up there, and it would be good for her. Elaine must find herself and has proven to be a fighter and smart as hell."

"What's going on up there?" I said, turning around to face him. I never really wore makeup, so a little eye shadow here and some lipstick, and I was good. That was Toya's thing.

"Shifter children are going missing. Quinn wants Kya and Kahlil to look into it, and I think Elaine would be a great help."

"Apu?" I asked. I knew this shit would start up again eventually.

"We don't know. Quinn is looking into it while I care for all this other bullshit. Listen, don't think about it right now. Go out and have fun. Don't let Toya get out there and start twerking all up on nobody. All we need is for True Alpha Quinn to lose his damn mind." I stood up with a big ass smile because I wasn't getting in the middle of that shit.

"I hear you," I said, moving to put on my clothes for the night.

It was a wrap ever since Cam showed Toya how to ride a motorcycle. She used that thing like it was nobody's business, driving Quinn crazy. He may have been throwing a fit, but I peeped at how he looked at her when she got off. All that "I need to speak to you privately" was bullshit. He banged that back out, and everyone knew it. I smiled as we both got off the bikes. The parking lot for the club was underground, and it was lit as hell. I mean, it was as if this was the club, but we knew differently.

"Oh, this is about to be fire!" Toya said over the noise of cars and other bikes. She knew she didn't have to speak loudly for me to hear her, but I guess it was still instinct.

"Hell yeah, and I can't wait to check this place out. Na'na said she put us on the list so we can bypass the long as fuck line." I said, pointing to the entrance. As we got closer, I saw the men Na'na always kept around. As I watched them, it was as if they moved between molecules or something. They were there, and then they weren't, and it made me blink fast. I had to know more about them or whatever the hell they were. I remember Michael saying they were called shadow people, but it had to be more to that story.

"Yeah, and that went well the last time our asses were put on "The List" in Florida." She said, using quotations like I wouldn't remember that bullshit.

"Well, this is different. We are family, and if they don't let us in, we can fuck shit up and push our way in." I said, laughing.

"Oh, that is what the hell I am talking about! I mean, look, I am even wearing some I will fuck you up shoes." We both burst out laughing as the tension and stress lessened somewhat. We haven't had a night like this in so long. I was just happy for whatever. Hell, we could stay in the parking lot. I looked around, seeing other supernaturals, and it was crazy to think we were part of this crowd. Hell, not that damn long ago, we thought we were human, and this shit never existed. I saw eyes flash, and some people had fucking tails. Various supernaturals out there are big, with too few tiny things buzzing around.

"Can you believe all this? How did we not know?" Toya said as we came up to the line. She was as wide-eyed just as I was.

"I have no idea," I said as we approached a black velvet rope with two tall, dark, lovely men. The one in front of us had a low cut, a mocha brown complexion, and glowing yellow eyes. His straight white teeth flashed when he spotted us.

"Well, damn," Toya said, looking him up and down. I mean, she had a point. My man was at least 6'3" and built like a tank. He was wearing an all-black suit like it was made for him.

"Ladies. My name is Tyson, and this is my associate, Ice, and he will take you to your table." His smooth deep voice sounded like sin, sex, and chocolate cake all rolled together as he smiled. I knew my mouth was open to say thank you, but Toya got to it first.

"Well, that is such a great service, Ty. Can I call you Ty?"

"Yes, you can." He laughed, letting us inside.

"Who the fuck are they?" I could hear someone ask.

"Damn, dude, shut the fuck up! If you don't know, get on the damn net and find out."

"Thank you, Tyson. I hope you have a good night." I said, smiling. Toya was already holding her hand out for Ice as we moved into an elevator with only one button, which was down.

Chapter Two

TARIA

As we stepped onto the elevator, I heard someone yell my name. I looked over at Toya, who heard it as well.

"Taria!" I turned back, looking at a woman I would have never believed would have been at this club. I moved when Ice held out a hand.

"Hold up." His British accent caught me off guard, and I heard Toya mumbling.

"Sexy as shit with an accent," she whispered as she looked at the shorter woman. "Isn't that Leila?" She asked as I placed a hand out to move Ice out of the way.

"I think so, but–"

"We should get in inside the club, Mrs. Vaughn." I looked up at the man like he was crazy as shit.

"Cross, but you can call me Taria," I said, smiling. "We can go to the club, but I need to see if this is who I think it is, and if so, she is coming with us," I said politely as possible, but the command in my voice was firm. His dark brown eyes flashed a lime green before a slow, sexy smile crossed his lips. He was tall, but only by a few inches to me. His dark brown skin was smooth except for the scar over his left eye. Ice also wore an all-black suit, but he wore a lime green tie. He also sported a low cut, which flowed into a goatee.

"You got that, Taria. I want to get you inside to start moving this line along." I nodded as I stepped back out of the elevator.

"Leila?" I said, walking closer. It looked like her, but I wasn't sure because the pointed ears, white hair, and golden markings on her face made her look slightly different. I couldn't deny the voice and attitude.

"Yeah! Who else would it be? Shit, I can't believe it is you. Hell, I thought all this shit going on was fake news or something, but—"

"Wait." I held up a hand, looking her over. She was always beautiful, in my opinion, with her golden-brown skin and delicate features, but now she looked as if she glowed. Her long moon-white hair was new, or was it her natural color? The markings on her face looked like a part of her skin. But I never saw her with pointed ears in all these years. I looked over at Tyson and nodded. He opened the rope, letting her through with some backlash until he snarled at the line.

"I am so happy to see you," she smiled with sharp white teeth.

"I... I don't even know what the fuck is going on," I said, leaning down to hug her. She smelled of flowers and Earth. "Listen, we must get into the club, so let's go. You can explain what the fuck is up with this pixie shit you got going on."

"Yeah, sure, no problem, but I am not one of those annoying as fuck pixies. I'm Elven. There is a big difference," Her soft voice said as she moved by me to hug Toya.

"Elves? Are you fucking kidding me?" I said, joining the three on the elevator. I looked at Ice as he hit the button, and the doors closed. He just chuckled at my face.

"Oh, baby girl, wait until you get inside. It's high time you get to know what else is out there." I turned back to look at the doors as Toya and Leila chatted. More fucking secrets to this paranormal bullshit. I felt a slight twitch in my stomach, and I knew my nerves were getting to me. I breathed deeply as the doors opened to slow, pulsating music.

"Ladies, please enjoy Sinful Secrets. The V.I.P. is across the room, and your reserved V.I.P. box is yours." Ice said, holding out a hand.

"Now, this is what a club should look like!" Toya said, grabbing my hand and leading me to the dance floor, with Leila following behind.

The club had different rooms, with each having its own style. I looked around as we danced to the music, and I could see some sups were watching me and others moving away from me. Our club room was lined with plush couches and red wine color with small tables throughout. The staff wore black from head to toe, which seemed like a high-class area. Everyone that wasn't dancing was drinking and talking over food I had never seen before in my life. I knew there had to be different rooms when I saw some walk-through with all leather or nothing at all and entered different doors. I looked toward the bar, and a beautiful woman caught my eye. She looked me over, and a smile crossed her lips as she nodded.

"Taria! We need to find our VIP box. We need to sit for a minute," Toya said, laughing.

"Yeah, we should catch up and check out the rest of this club. I heard it was like seven or eight different rooms." Leila said as she moved her long blue locks from her face. The white markings on her face moved slightly. They were both right. We needed to talk and check this place out because Na'na had been holding back.

"Yeah, yeah, let's do that," I said, returning to the bar and seeing the woman was gone. I felt I should know who she was, but I never saw her before. The energy was familiar, but I knew I had never met that woman a day in my life. I looked for the V.I.P. section and saw a man standing next to some stairs with another black velvet rope. "Come on. I think that is what Ice was talking about." As we pushed through the crowd, I felt something brush along my legs, and I looked down.

"Did you feel that?" Toya said, looking around and down at her feet.

"Yeah, I did."

"What the hell are you two talking about?" Leila looked at us like we were trippin' or something.

"You didn't feel something brush along your legs?" I asked. I didn't hear her response as I tuned everything and everyone out. I blinked slowly, letting my eyes glow white as I saw a black cloud clinging to Toya's legs. I could feel my fangs descend fast while I lifted my thumb to my mouth, spilling my blood. I hissed as I reached out and grabbed the slippery substance touching my friend.

"What the fuck!" Toya yelled as every eye landed on us three. I let my eyes return to normal, trying to figure out how I just did that and what the fuck this shit was.

"Oh shit. How the hell did you do that? Shit, where did that come from?" Leila said, looking around.

"Was that shit on me?" Toya said as she started checking her body for more of it. It wasn't a demon. That much was for sure, but it was dark.

"Someone or something is trying to attach itself to you." A soft voice said as the music played once more. The woman from the bar approached us as Toya stopped her fidgeting, and her eyes turned blue-green. Before the woman could say more, Toya approached me, chanting fast and low. She reached out for the darkness with a handful of fire. Her words and fire engulfed the substance along with my hand. I expected pain from the fire but felt nothing as the black shit disintegrated.

"Such power for a young Witch." We all looked at the woman standing before us with narrowed eyes. She was so lovely with her cinnamon-brown complexion and long dark brown hair that fell to her back. Her cat-like eyes followed my every movement as I put myself before LaToya and Leila.

"Who are you?" I asked as I felt Toya push herself from behind me to stand next to me.

"Yeah, who the hell are you, and how did you know what that shit was trying to do?" Toya asked, raising her brows high on her forehead. The woman looked over at Toya with a quick flip of her eyes and then turned back to me.

"You shouldn't go around just touching things. You don't know what it is."

"Ahh, hell naw bitch," Toya said as the woman dismissed her. I could feel Toya's power growing, but I put out a hand to calm her. She side-eyed me like I was losing my damn mind, but she bit down on her tongue to keep quiet. This woman was powerful and old as fuck, but I couldn't shake the feeling that I should know who or what the fuck she was or what she was.

"Maybe I shouldn't, but I won't let any harm come to the people I care about or people I am charged with protecting," I said.

"So self-righteous. It reminds me of someone I knew. Someone I thought I would never see again. You even remind me of her." I noticed other supernaturals were moving away but keeping close just to see what the fuck was about to go down.

"Well, she must be someone I would love to meet, but never mind all this bullshit. Who the hell are you, and what do you know about the shit that attacked my friend?" This woman was making me uneasy. I wouldn't say I liked the way she was looking at me. I felt she had something to do with what was also trying to attack Toya.

"Taria, Taria, is that any way for you to speak to your aunt? You did have something to do with my son's death." Her deep growl rolled out of her throat. I could see her hands shifting, but she controlled herself. Everyone here knew this club was neutral ground, and if you didn't abide by the rules, the punishment was severe — no matter who the hell you were.

"Don't fucking tell me this bitch is Justin's mother," Toya said wide-eyed. She stared hard into my eyes, and I knew she could see the flashes of lightning. She sucked in a quick breath but said nothing.

"So, Masika, have you come here to avenge your son?" I asked as my palm itched for a blade. She cocked her head to the side as she watched me. Her skin rippled over her flesh, and my fangs grew longer, readying myself for a fight. Fuck the rules. I knew what this bitch was about and what she and her punk ass mother tried to do to mine.

"You should have never been born in the first damn place. So, life for life seems fair enough for me. After I finish with you, I will handle my sister just as we would have before your father stepped in."

"Not in my fucking club!" We all looked to the stairs where the voice came from. Shannara, in all her succubus glory, came down the steps. One of her shadow men was in front of her. The other was behind her, but she didn't need them. I have seen Na'na in action, but looking at her now, my mouth fell open. She wore a long white silk dress that clung to her body... I didn't know how the hell it still fit her with this transformation, but it did.

"The only way that dress is still on is because of a spell. I am telling you, Taria, because ain't no fucking way." Toya whispered beside me. I had no idea how she knew exactly what the hell I was thinking. I watched as Na'na approached us with her clawed hands balled into a fist. Her horns flowed down her back as her light blue eyes scanned the room. Her long tail whipped back and forth, making everyone move out of her way. "Hello, Auntie." She hissed as her fangs grew longer than mine.

NA'NA

I couldn't believe she thought she could show her ass in my damn club. Then have the fucking nerve to speak to my cousin as if she thought she would take her out. These bitches still don't know or understand her mother, nor will I ever let that happen. As I approached them, I could feel all eyes on us when I spoke. Everyone and their mother knew this was not the place for violence. I wasn't with that, and this spot was neutral on the pain of death.

"Everyone knows the rules to my fucking club, and just because you are family doesn't excuse you from it." I snapped. My blue laser gaze fell onto Taria and Toya, making sure there wasn't any harm done to them, but I knew I couldn't let that attack on the stand.

"Family? You are no family of mine. You are nothing but a succubus bitch who should have never been allowed to be born in the first place," Masika growled. I was never going to be accepted as part of the panther shifter race, and I already came to terms with that. Not to mention, I knew the lies I told myself about my parents only blocked the pain of never being wanted.

"Well, good, then that makes this much easier," I said as the two shadow men by my side stepped forward. "You can either leave by paying the fine for disobeying my rules or suffer punishment. "You cast a spell in my club that tried to harm another. You can pay or–" I held my hand, letting my claws lengthen.

"I will not pay for shit! It wasn't me who cast that spell, so you need to find the right one. Also, let your mother know we are also here for her." I looked her over, not seeing the black marking that would appear on her skin if she broke a rule. She was right about that, but she would have had a knockdown drag-out fight with Taria if I hadn't stepped in.

"My mother was cast aside when your mother found out Bast also slept with my grandmother. She has done nothing but escapes your and your mother's way. Leave her the fuck out of this. You have a problem, I can fucking settle it, but it won't be here in my place of business. Now get the fuck out." The two men at my side blurred as they moved forward.

"This isn't finished," Masika snapped at Taria and glared at me as she moved quickly before the shadows could touch her. No one wanted their touch or could handle it. They move between this world and the afterlife. Them touching you is like touching death. You may not like what you see or feel. Taria watched the woman with flashing eyes as she pushed past the onlookers. I looked around, and others looked away quickly, and the music started up again.

"Sorry, Na'na." Taria sighed as she shook her head.

"You good. They were bound to show their faces soon enough. I didn't think she would have the balls to do it here," I said. Toya was still looking at me with her mouth open, and others were. I don't normally transform, but the staring always follows when I do.

"Well, you three, have a good night. I need to make my rounds to ensure everyone follows my rules." I said, raising my voice at the end.

"I feel you, cuz. Hey, stop by the house tomorrow. I want to speak to you about something. More like a favor for your favorite cousin." Taria smiled. I would have smiled back, but I was sure my smile in this form would scare the shit out of everyone in here. So, I just nodded before turning and disappearing into the crowd.

Chapter Three

TARIA

I knew Toya was about to comment, so I turned to her with a smile.

"Spit it out," I said, looking at her open mouth.

"I don't know if I should be afraid or aroused. The feeling is weird as fuck, and I am guessing that's just one of her powers?" She said, shaking her head.

"Shannara, is your cousin?" Leila asked. I looked over at her, taking in her looks again, and shook my head.

"Yes, she is, but I think we should hear way more about you, Leila." I smiled as we pushed through the crowd to get to our table. After entering the V.I.P. lounge, I looked around and caught a few eyes looking our way. Toya stuck her finger in the air, and a tall, slender woman dressed in black approached with a tray of drinks.

"My name is Tasha, and I will care for you ladies tonight. Na'na says the first round is on her." The woman smiled as she put three large wine glasses before us.

"Thank you, Tasha," I said as she stood back up.

"Thank you, my Queen." I saw Toya smirk out of the corner of my eye as I smiled at the waitress.

"You can call me Taria. Thank you again for the drinks." She flashed a quick smile as she flashed away quickly out of sight.

"You said I need to start talking? What about you two because? I damn sure didn't see this shit coming?" Leila laughed as we sipped our wine.

"Damn, this shit is good," Toya said. I could taste the blood laced in my wine, which had me lifting an eyebrow in surprise. I sat my glass down and turned to Leila.

"Well, I think you should go first." I smiled. I was looking at Leila, but I could see Toya out of the corner of my eye, drawing something on the table as she looked herself over.

"What is there to tell? I am a Moon Elf or Silver Elf." She laughed lightly. There was so much more out there, making me wonder about everyone I knew. Who was human, and who wasn't? Everything I thought I knew was a lie, but the truth slowly revealed itself.

"So, how many different types of elves is it?" I asked. I felt Toya stiffen, and it had me on alert. "What's wrong?" I said, turning to face her.

"Nothing. It's cool, and it's cool," she said, loosening her body.

"Naw. What are you thinking?" I asked as I scanned the room. I caught sight of a tall woman slipping out of the door on the side, and I stood.

"No! Taria, chill out. I can handle this. This isn't the place or time right now."

"What the hell is going on?" I could feel my fangs wanting out and feel the strike of lightning inside my body.

"That attack wasn't about your people. It was toward me from my people or, more so, one of my aunt's followers. I'm on guard now, but I will handle my business."

"Shit, we can handle this shit right now," I said, ready to end the bullshit. Ever since Toya went to that damn meeting with those Witch bitches, it's been one thing after another. At least some have joined her, but others were on the dumb shit I wasn't with.

"I got this girl. This is the problem that I will handle. You have enough on your plate, and we are supposed to have fun tonight." Toya smiled and lifted a hand for another drink.

"Aight, I feel you on that, but you know when you need me—"

"Yeah, yeah, Taria. I know to call you. Just handle your shit, ok? I got this." Tasha came back to the table with a smile and six-shot glasses.

"This is from the human sitting at the bar." I saw a flash of fang when Tasha flicked her eyes to the bar. As she sat the drinks down, I looked over and saw Agent Jason Davis.

"Aww, shit!" Toya said, taking a shot back to back. Leila looked around and saw who Tasha was pointing out and looked at me.

"Who the hell is that?"

"Girl, if Michael finds out he is here—"

"Shut the hell up, Toya. I didn't know he was going to be here tonight."

"Yeah, ok, and Michael is going to care because—" I rolled my eyes as I took one shot before I stood to make my way to the bar.

"Toya, who the hell is it?" Leila asked again.

"Girl... long story. Let me start from when we went on a vacation." I heard Toya say before I drowned her out. I knew she was filling Leila in on what happened these past months, but I still wanted more out of Leila about Elves. I would need to know all I could if I was going to deal with this royal bullshit. I would finish my questions later because I needed to find out why Jason was here and who the hell let him in.

Michael

I knew things were about to get real and soon as fuck. I just hoped Taria was up for this challenge, even though I know she wanted to square shit away with this Hunter mess. Her father was ready to go off and find Beverly before she started an all-out war between the families. I knew for a fucking fact Taria didn't want him to leave, and her mother wasn't having that shit. Not unless she went with him this time. I knew we had that shit to work out, but the fact that I had to hold a trial this week brought every High Blue Blood vampire to Maryland. Yes, we were crowned, but the formal ceremony would take place in the upcoming days since everyone was getting together.

I was glad Camron didn't kill Sara Van Allan because maybe I could get some answers to why her husband and brother-in-law would use a demon against his own. It couldn't have been all about power. It had to be something more. Also, I knew some Blue Bloods still disagreed or did not believe Peter and his sons should have been murdered and believed Taria was the reason behind it.

"Damn, I thought I had a lot of shit on my mind," Quinn said as he walked into my office. He held Reign in his right arm, carrying a large book in the other.

"Yeah, too much shit. Fuck it, what's up?" I asked as I leaned back into my chair. I watched as Quinn placed the book on the table and sat before me.

"How the hell am I supposed to unite all the wolf shifters? I already have some Alphas not recognizing me as their True Alpha. I don't have time to go to each pack and rip these bitches' heads off." I wanted to laugh my ass off because, as he said this shit, he had a burping cloth over his shoulder as he patted Reign's back lightly.

"Why do you need to be the one to do it? You are the True Alpha, and just as you sent Hayley to handle your old pack in Florida, you sent someone else to hand out your orders." He sat thinking about my words as Reign let out a loud burp. The little girl kept squirming until Quinn stood and handed her to me. I picked her up, kissing my niece on the cheek as she smiled.

"You do know that your kids are way too fucking aware of shit," I said as Quinn sat back down.

"Yeah, I know. It's cool. We got this handled." He looked at the book before turning his dark eyes back to mine. "I found this in Colleen's things. She had a page marked in the book, and I thought I should tell you about this. I need to bring these packs to heel because something is coming, and it will take us all to beat this shit."

I looked down at Reign as she closed her eyes and drifted off to sleep, even with the room full of tension.

"Read it to me, Quinn," I said, not really wanting to hear another fucking problem.

"Aight. So, most of this book talks about the Royal families of wolf shifter packs, but then this shit goes sideways on some prophecy shit." I watched as he flipped to the page that Colleen had marked.

"When the True Alpha comes again, and a world-ending battle takes place, the seal will break. IT will rise from the depths claim-

ing all life once more. Unite as one or die as a whole as the world succumbs to darkness. The True Alpha must unite his wolves, just as the Vampire King must control his throne, Hunters must maintain the balance of good and evil. A new circle of Witches will form, starting a new High Council as the fire breathers will rise again."

I had him read it two more times before I nodded. We knew something was coming. Now was the time to get ahead. I was glad we sent Marcus and Na'na on this mission because something told me time was of the essence. What had my eyes glowing was the mention of fire breathers. I couldn't understand what it could mean because my grandmother was the last dragon anyone had ever seen and was dead.

"Quinn, you need to find your way, and I know you will, but you also need to trust in your Alphas to make the ones who fight your rule bow down to you. Find out what or who corrupts your wolves, and everything else will work out." I saw him taking in my words, and I could tell he was working through some things.

"I got you. I need to call together all the Alphas. Even the ones who don't believe I am what I am. I think it's about time for them to understand who their Alpha is." Quinn stood, and so did I, to hand the baby back over to him. I knew that he and Toya had to take their own journey so we could all be ready for whatever the fuck IT was. Quinn picked up his book and started for the door when it opened to Garrett and Lily.

"Daddy!" Quinn just smiled as Garrett rushed after Lily.

"Lily, you are supposed to be in bed!" Garrett screamed over Lily's giggling.

"Lily, why are you giving your brother a hard time? Princesses are supposed to be sleeping."

"I know, Daddy, but I had a dream."

"Ok, about what? You can tell me while I take you back to your room before you get in trouble with your mother."

"Don't tell her," she whispered.

"Tell me what the dream was about," I said instead.

"Well, it was so hot! Like fire hot. I wasn't burning or anything."

"Then how was it fire hot, Lily," Garrett asked, rolling his eyes.

"Because it was Gar! She was asleep, but she is waking now and needs help. I told her my daddy could help anybody. I told her you were a King, and you and my mommy could fix anything. She said that she was hurt really bad and that I should come to find her."

"Ok, wait!"

"What, Daddy? I told her I couldn't because I was too small and couldn't go that far yet, but she could see me then when I got older and married."

"Hold up! First, you are not growing up anytime soon, and second, you will never have a boyfriend or get married!" I was done. Hell, no, my baby girl wasn't getting married or having a boyfriend.

"Oh my God, Lily! It was a dream, just like the man with the rainbow eyes is a dream." Garrett said as he walked to his room and closed the door. I looked back at Lily and saw her drop her head down. DAMN! I got down on one knee and lifted her head to see her eyes.

"I know that you are very special, Lily. I also know that your dreams are more than what they should be. It is just right now, you are too young to understand them fully. So whatever dream you have, you can always come to tell me, and we will figure it out together. Even if it's about you having a boyfriend." Her little arms came around my neck, but she didn't know that as soon as I found out who these boys were, I would take care of that shit way before she ever thought about a boyfriend.

"I love you, Daddy, but I will only have one boyfriend." She kissed my cheek and entered her room, closing her door behind her.

"Aww, fuck this shit. The first Rainbow colored eyed dude comes through here. I am fucking them up on sight." I stood, taking a deep breath as I headed for my mother's room. It was time to pull her shit together because the covens were coming.

Chapter Four

JASON

I couldn't believe how easy it was to get inside this club. I knew Shannara Cane owned a few clubs around this city, but we could never get inside. I should have known something was up when it wasn't a problem this time around. I felt a chilly hand on my shoulder before I could send over some drinks to Taria and her friends. I turned, not seeing anyone, but I could feel the cold sinking into my skin, making me feel as if death was creeping its way into my body.

"You are here because Taria wouldn't want anything to happen to those she calls a friend, and my mistress allowed you to enter this place. Your badge won't work here, so don't fuck up, or I will throw you the fuck out. Friend or no friend." The coldness was gone as the bartender approached me, looking at me like I was suspicious. He looked like he was half bull, half man, but who the fuck was I to judge. Ever since that battle, I have seen all kinds of fucked up shit.

"Can you give their waitress six shots of Patron on me?" I said, pointing at the table Taria and her friends were sitting and laughing. The snort had my eyes turning back to the bartender.

"Do you know who they are?" The deep, gruff voice sounded like falling rocks when he spoke.

"Yeah, I do. Can you handle that order?" I said, putting down five twenties.

"Your life." He snorted again as he grabbed up the cash, and I was sure I would see hoofs instead of hands. I returned to the bar and sipped on my Henny while the waitress took my drinks. I felt my phone vibrating, so I reached into my pocket to pull it out. Looking at the screen, I saw a blocked number and knew it was the job.

"Davis," I answered as I lifted my drink to my lips again. Damn, that shit was good and smooth.

"Agent Davis. I was hoping you could set up a meeting with that bloodsucker friend of yours. Someone or thing broke into our facility and stole our prisoner. Agents are dead, and the higher-ups want answers and someone to pay for the fuck up." These people were fucking crazy as hell if they thought Taria would meet on our terms again. I also knew they didn't know we had one of their people held to be studied. Shit, I just found out and was against that shit. The president wanted peace between the species, but they just had to study shit they didn't understand. They were predators and killers. It was always a mistake on their part to take that boy from that night.

"All I can do is extend the invitation."

"You get her to agree to a meet, Davis! Our jobs depend on it. We need to make them believe we were trying to help him before whoever took him gets to them first. They need to trust us, Davis, until we—"

"Sir, I will do what I can. We shouldn't be having this conversation where I am in."

"How did you get in?" He knew I was somewhere every one of his agents tried to infiltrate.

"Honestly, I don't know."

"Check out what you can and get some pictures if possible. I want a full report about that place first thing, Davis! Make it happen. We need to speak to her again." The call ended, and I stuck it back into my pocket and picked up my drink once again. I turned so I could see the table once more and almost choked. Taria was slipping through the crowd, heading directly toward me. Her eyes were a glowing brown, and her luscious body moving had me rearranging myself.

"Jason, what are you doing here?" She asked with a slight smile on her lips. I could see the tips of her fangs, but it didn't take away from her thick thighs, large breast, smooth brown skin, and kissable lips. I cleared my throat as she bit down on her bottom lip and raised an eyebrow.

"I wanted to see what it was all about. What are you doing here?"

"Minding my business and trying to have some fun for once." She shrugged. I scanned the room, catching a few glares, and some hissed at me.

"I don't think they fuck with me up in here." I laughed but ensured I had my shit just in case something popped off. I was surprised I didn't even get checked for anything.

"Well, maybe you shouldn't be here. I hope you're not digging for information here or following me."

"Now, why would I do something that fucking crazy, and you're welcome for the drinks?"

"I didn't ask for them, so I didn't see the need to thank you."

"Oh, damn. Someone has a sharp tongue." She shook her head and looked around as a Cardi B song played.

"Taria, let's go! This is my shit!" She turned away when I reached out, grabbing her arm.

"Wait." She pulled, and my grip broke easily, reminding me exactly who and what she was.

"Yes."

"Are you willing to meet with me and my superiors again?" She scoffed.

"I knew you were on some shit," she said, turning to leave.

"Naw, I'm serious. This is important, Taria. This could help build a bridge between worlds. We also have some information, one vampire that we were trying to help." Her brows drew down as she faced me fully.

"What the fuck are you talking about? What vampire could you have helped?"

"One that was hurt while you were battling. A young man by the name of Luke." I watched her eyes lit with an intense glow, and I could have sworn white flashes burned in her eyes.

"I will contact you with a place and time. If your bosses don't like it, then you can tell them I said I don't give a fuck. I don't know what game is being played, Jason, but I hope you have nothing to do with it." She turned on her heel so fast I didn't even realize she was halfway across the floor until someone touched my arm. I looked over, seeing the waitress that gave Taria and her crew their drinks were glaring at me. I watched as her fangs descended, and she growled at me.

"I think it is time for you to leave," she hissed as her grip became unbreakable.

"It's a free fucking country. I don't have to do shit."

"Let me rephrase what the hell I just said. My King thinks it is time for you to leave." I watched her eyes for a moment and saw she wasn't lying. I pulled my arm away and drank the last bit of my Henny before I answered her.

"Tell your King I already got what I needed, anyway." I slammed the glass back on the bar and turned to leave. I took one more look toward Taria as she moved to the music. She may be a vampire now, but she was still human at heart, and I guess that was what most attracted me to her. I turned and got the hell out of there before I ended up as someone's fucking dinner.

Taria

I knew something wasn't right, but I kept dancing anyway. Toya would be leaving soon to handle her business, and I needed to find out what Hunters were on my side and who was riding with that bitch Beverly. I wouldn't say shit about Jason being here tonight, but his last words had my mind racing. Luke was alive, and the government had him. I don't care what they say. I know for a fucking fact they were studying him, not to mention what they could have learned from his blood. Michael had to know this, especially before the trial of Sara Van Allan. Luke is a Blue Blood and still a child in the older vampire's eyes. Losing him will not look good on Michael, and I knew meeting up with these government assholes would give me more answers.

"You're a fucking Hunter?" Leila said with a trace of fear in her eyes when she realized I was back. It hurt somewhat that she would think I would hurt her, but I understood somewhat why.

"Whatever you have been told about Hunters isn't right, but that is a story for another time," I said, dancing and trying to squeeze some fun into tonight. The club music got louder as the crowd grew, and more bodies hit the floor.

"That is a story I think I should hear. If what I am hearing is true, my elders may want an audience with you and your King." I watched the markings on her skin move along as she danced, but I could see the seriousness in her eyes. I could also see this wasn't the place to hold this conversation.

"I got you. Let's just enjoy tonight and figure the bullshit out tomorrow," I said, pulling out my phone to text Michael about the Luke shit. I slipped my phone back into my pocket and lost myself in the music. Tomorrow real-life shit starts, and we must get a handle on it soon or face another battle we may not win this time.

KATHERINE

I knew I had locked myself up long enough in this room, but I couldn't pull myself out of my misery. All those years, Victor held me captive. My mind only focused on staying alive to save my sons. I stayed alive just to feel the loss and pain of losing another child out of my life. This time was different because I didn't have my husband, my *Kindred Soul,* by my side to see me through this. I could feel a touch of sunlight hit my arm from the window where the curtains were left partially open. I heard voices outside my room and laughter from children I still hadn't met. My grandchildren wanted to meet me, but I couldn't move. A light knock hit my door, but I wouldn't remove the spell I laid over it. When the door opened, I guess it didn't matter if I did or didn't.

"Mother." It was Michael, my last living son and the one to look most like his father. He even sounded like him, if not slightly deeper. "Mother, I know you can hear me." I felt the bed dip as he sat next to me. I couldn't open my mouth or move, but I only wanted to hold him tight. "I am going to say this once. You have two grandchildren waiting to see you and others who missed you and want to see you. I have accepted what fate has dealt with me, and I am King. That said, I will give you one day to pull your shit together and become the strong woman I know you to be. I have the information you may want to hear and have found things I need to know more about. So that being said, Mother, as your King, you will get your shit together." I could feel the command in my blood pushing me to move, but what made my mouth open wasn't because he ordered me to. It was because he thought he could. I moved swiftly, opening the curtains to let the sunlight hit me fully. I heard him stand, and I turned toward my son.

"King or not, Michael, you are still my child, and I will be damned if you order me to do anything. Also, watch your damn mouth and tone when you speak to me!" The house shook to the foundation as a large smile formed on his lips. "I know you are King, and Taria will be Queen, but I am still Queen until the official ceremony occurs! I am a ruler in your father's place until I hand our people over to you. I will only say that once." I had no idea where I gained the strength to stand or speak.

"Good because the Blue Bloods will be arriving very soon. We have a lot of things to go over in a short time, Mother. It's good to know I can count on you to stand beside me." His words hit my heart with pain because I hadn't been there for him and was hiding away instead of helping my remaining son.

"Give me a day, Michael. Just give me a day."

"I would give you longer if I could. We don't have that time." He took two quick steps toward me. His large arms hugged me close, and I knew this pity shit had to end. I couldn't feel Micah, but I didn't feel him pass on either.

"I love you, son." He kissed my cheek and left the room. I stood in the sunlight and could feel the rays soaking into my skin. My blood hummed as I heard a whisper of a voice I shouldn't be able to hear.

"Mother... I am not dead."

I turned to look behind me, but no one was there. I knew that voice because it was one a mother would never forget. It had to be him, but how and why now?

"Jessiah?"

Chapter Five

TARIA

I can honestly say it was nice as hell not to wake up with a hangover. I noticed that I had two other people besides me on the bed.

"Taria, it's too early for you to be up!" Toya groaned. I guess she still can get hungover. It sucks for her because we had to get up.

"It's not as early as you think it is, Toya," I said as I looked for my phone. I peeled open my other eye and saw Lily smiling in my face while holding my phone.

"Aunt Toya, it's almost noon! The babies have been up already, and Uncle Quinn has been running around like he's crazy." Lily laughed.

"Lily, give Mommy her phone and stop yelling, please."

"Oh shit! We are leaving soon, and I am not ready!" Toya said, jumping up.

"Will, all of you, shut up!" I looked at the bottom of the bed and saw long white hair over an arm covered in white hair.

"Hey, elf lady, that is not a nice word!" Lily said, stomping her foot.

"Lily, I thought I told you to leave them alone." Michael's smooth, deep voice sent tingles down my body. The bed jostled as Toya launched herself out of bed, almost tripping but catching herself.

"Shit, shit, shit. Sorry, Lily." Toya bent down and kissed her head as she ran out of the room. "Quinn, why didn't you wake me up? I don't even know what shoes I am going to wear."

I sat up, looking at Michael as Lily ran out of the room, yelling for Uncle Marcus. I felt the bed move again and looked at Leila, peeking under the blankets.

"Ahh... Taria is that—" She pointed a finger to Michael as she mouthed the word, King.

"Yeah, it's cool."

"Oh, God!" She screamed into the pillow.

"I thought Moon Elves were more diplomatic?" Michael said with a half-smile.

"Leave her alone," I said, getting to my feet. "Leila, take your time and get yourself together. Come downstairs when you're ready. There is a bathroom with fresh linen and clothes that should fit you. We have a lot to talk about, I am guessing." All I got back was a shaky laugh.

"Aight, you got that. Just give me a few to pull my shit together."

"No worries, girl, it's cool. Just don't take it all day. I have a feeling shit is about to start moving rather quickly." I started for the door with Michael pressed behind me.

"I think you're right on that one, sweetheart, but you forgot to tell me something last night." I had to think back, and I was damn sure I said something about Jason.

"Oh, you talking about Masika." I opened the doors to our room and stripped so I could jump in the shower before Toya had to leave.

"Yeah, about that. Don't you think after that shit went down, you should have brought your ass home or fucking called?" I turned on the water and stepped in under the hot spray. I didn't want to look at him because I knew those eyes were glowing fiery gold. I was about to apologize when I realized I didn't tell him, so how the fuck did he know?

"Wait! How the hell did you know she showed up last night?" I turned around then because I was mad as hell. I knew his ass had someone following me. I didn't know who the hell it was. When I faced him, he was already undressed and getting into the shower with me. He moved so fast that I didn't realize he had me backed up against the wall.

"I have eyes everywhere, Taria. It doesn't matter what you say or how fucking mad you get. I will always make sure you are safe and that I know what the fuck is going on when it comes to you." I had something on the tip of my tongue, but I sucked in a breath as he slowly let his big hands slide across my shoulders lightly until he had a handful of my breasts. I could feel him hard against me as his eyes held mine.

"This isn't fair. I can take care of myself," I said. He didn't reply as he kissed and licked me on my neck.

"Shit..." I moaned. He slid his hands between my thighs, arousing my clit as my nipples hardened.

"I am just going to take this moment because I don't know when we will have another like this again." He growled as he leaned down, biting into my neck. It was as if I hadn't felt this feeling in so long. "Damn..." He pulled away but licked my throat when I felt his hands on my waist. He spun me around and pushed me up against the shower wall. The water ran down my hair and onto my back as he slid straight into my tight space. "Baby..." I gasped out of pure fulfillment of his presence inside of me.

"I got you, sweetheart," he said as he grew inside me with each pump. I tried to stand straight back up when he bent me back over, putting his hand on the middle of my back, and I felt his other hand slide around to my stomach. He pushed in deeper, and I could feel my legs begin to shake. I knew he was right, and we may not get another minute like this, and I wouldn't waste it. I pushed back, forcing him to take a step back and slide out of me so I could turn around. I finally took some control, but it was lost as he pushed me back against the shower wall.

"Damn, baby," I moaned. Michael leaned down, taking my lips, but I pulled away when I felt my fangs lengthen.

"You don't hurt me, Taria. Do it!" He growled as I leaned in, sinking my fangs in me while his fingers found my clit once more. It felt like a hot fire in my veins but it didn't burn me. It felt like pure power, and I wanted more. I returned for another bite, but he held me back with a small smile.

"Too much power won't be good for the baby." His words filtered through my lust, hazed mind.

"Wait. What?" I said when he slowly kneeled on his knees and guided my leg over his shoulder. With my back against the wall, he held me in the perfect position to get a taste of me. I thought I would climb up the walls while my legs shook and my eyes rolled in the back of my head.

"I... I didn't forget—" I tried to say, but I lost it when his tongue flicked my sensitive nerves. He slowly moved upward, kissing every inch of my body all the way back up to my neck, where his fangs sank in deep again. He didn't drink long, but the feeling from his fangs was as if he fucked me all over again. He pulled back, staring me in the eyes, and his golden gaze burned into my soul. I could feel the connection, the love, and the fact I would do anything to keep him safe and to stay by his side.

I grabbed his face, and he stuck my tongue in his mouth. He pulled back because I could feel exactly what he was feeling.

"Finish up here, and we will continue this again." His spicy scent and voice made me do a whole-body shudder as he left the shower.

"I won't be long," I called out. I could feel the two bitches and the rest of his crew getting close. Needless to say, my legs were shaking so badly after he left out of the bathroom, I found myself stuck in position leaning against the wall. I looked down, where my hand rested on my stomach, and shook my head.

"Naw, he got to be fucking with me." I shook my head again, reaching over for my body wash so we could start the day and the bullshit.

Coming down the stairs, I didn't know where everyone went, but I was glad not to see the two vamp bitches. I know one or both of them hoes slept with Michael. He might not think I know about that shit, but I can read the lust, and jealousy that rolls off of both of them. He may trust them, but I damn sure didn't and wouldn't have them watch my back if the Hunters were coming on one side and my deranged family from my mother's side was coming from the other. My phone beeped, and I looked at the message from Na'na, saying she was on her way. She must have got my voicemail this morning. I said ok and put my phone back in my jeans pocket. I heard a very cultured deep rumble coming down the next hall, so I stopped and stood to the side. I knew it was

Marcus, but something told me not to interrupt his call. I had to listen in because he was just so damn quiet and uptight. Plus, his ass always puts me through the bullshit when training, so I needed something on his ass. He had to be preoccupied because he should have sensed me.

"Mother, how are you?" I heard him ask. He had to be leaving Michael's office and had just got the news of his new adventure.

"Marcus! Don't be flip with me, boy. What is going on out there? Things are getting out of hand. What is Michael planning on doing about this whole human thing?" I had to roll my eyes and could tell his mother was going to be overdramatic about every damn thing. I just hoped she wasn't one I had to watch out for. I am going to need everyone I can get.

"Mother, please. Everything will be fine, but right now, I cannot talk. Michael needs me for a mission, and I must prepare." Marcus said in his clipped tone. God, he looked so much like Cam's sexy ass, but they were nothing alike in personality. Marcus was good people, though. "What! You can't go on a mission with such chaos happening. That girl he is running around with is causing a scene." I know she isn't talking about me. I moved so he could see me when I heard a slight growl.

"That girl is named Taria, Mother, and she is our Queen. Once you meet her, you will understand, so don't judge. Honestly, she and Cam are close, and I now see why. She is like a sister, but I won't tell her that." It took me back a step the way he spoke up for me. I stood there in disbelief.

"Sister?" I heard his mother ask.

I heard him come to a stop and saw him stop outside Katherine's room. He placed a hand on her door, and I could feel the pain and sadness coming off of him.

"Did the rumors you heard tell you Katherine is alive?" He asked as he pushed himself from the door.

"What! Are you telling me that is true?" I could hear the happiness and sadness in his mother's voice. Shit, maybe she wasn't all that bad. I would have to see when I met her.

"Yes, ma'am, that is true."

"We need to visit. I have to talk to your father about this. I want the entire story. We both want to hear the full story." The call ended. I stepped out from the corner, smiled, and leaned against the wall.

"So, I'm like a sista?" I smiled wider, showing fangs.

"Yes, a sister who has been trying to skip out on training. Let's go!" My mouth fell open as he moved past me with a smile.

"Wait, a minute!" I didn't have time for this. I tried reaching out to Michael, mind to mind, but the asshole blocked me. I was going to kick his damn ass.

"Nope, too late! Let's move Taria Cross. I want short sword exercises blindfolded." I followed, grumbling to myself. Before we hit the back door, I could feel the overwhelming presence of my cousin coming to save me from the bullshit.

"Hello, Marcus." I heard Na'na say, but I watched as Marcus looked at her starting from her toes, and followed her curves to her face. Aww, shit, now this is going to be good!

"Shannara, it is always a pleasure to see you," Marcus answered while licking his lips. Man, the sexual tension between the two of them was off the damn hook.

I followed their verbal sparring match until I caught Na'na looking at me with a death glare. I cleared my throat to speak.

"Ahh, Marcus. This really won't take long, and I will be right..."

"Naw, sis. If Shannara wants to talk, then she can wait or join. I know her kind always likes to get her way, but that shit isn't happening today." I closed my mouth when the back and forth started again. I didn't know who was more turned on, Marcus or Na'na. Shit, who was tempting who?

Na'na moved quickly, grabbing me by the arm. I knew he could catch us if he wanted, but his laugh told me he knew exactly what she would do.

"Na'na, what the hell?" I said when we stopped at the edge of my property.

We stood next to the gate entrance that surrounded acres of my land. She was breathing hard. I don't think she should have been.

"Sorry. He just gets under my damn skin. He looks at me like he could handle what I have to... never mind. Tell me about this damn mission you want me to go on, and why the hell does he need to go?" She said, raising her voice slightly at the end. I eyed her like she was crazy. I knew damn well she never got flustered or tongue-tied around anyone.

"Humm. Ok, if that is how you want to play this. I need to know what the hell that mermaid was talking about. I have so much going on right now that I don't have time to hunt for her. I didn't have time to hunt for answers right now. Shit is getting crazy with people figuring out this supernatural shit is real life, and the whole becoming Queen shit is off the damn hook." She reached out, pulling me into a hug, using her chi to push happiness and love into my soul. I felt my shoulders relax, and I gave her my weight. I didn't know I was so tense about all this shit.

"You know I got you, Taria. Anything you need from me, I will do my best to get it done."

"Thank you, Na'na." I pulled back, smiling at her like a fool. "So, what the hell was that shit with Marcus? I mean, the sexual tension between the two of you was HOT AS HELL." I thought she would put me in a headlock like when we were younger.

"Fuck you," she said and started back toward the house. I laughed at her, but I knew she liked him. Hell, maybe she would be the only one to tame the King's Blade.

Chapter Six

TARIA

"That is enough. Five-minute breaks, then I want each of you to pair up and spar." I heard Marcus yell across the yard. I saw Garrett put his blade away before he came running over to Na'na and me.

"Mom, shouldn't you be resting or something?" Garrett asked after hugging Na'na tightly. Everyone knew exactly what she was and kept their distance except Garrett and Lily. My two babies were unique in their own way. I looked down at Garrett as his words hit me.

"Garrett, I am not an old lady. I chilled out today, but your Uncle Marcus thinks I must train, so here I am." I said, leaning down to kiss him.

"Come on, Mom, everyone is out here," Garrett grumbled. I smiled at him as another heated conversation started between Marcus and Na'na. Before I could tell both of them it was time to chill the fuck out, they went at it. We all sat there with mouths open. I looked around and saw a few vamps and shifters looking shocked as hell. It was over before anyone could stop it, though. Marcus looked around and shook his head.

"Everyone pair up and spar!" Marcus said as everyone scrambled. Shit, I was, too, because he was a damn drill instructor. Garrett ran back to his partner, and I looked around when I felt my phone start to vibrate. I pulled it out, seeing a text from Jason.

"I hope you are not going to stand me up?" I looked at the message but didn't respond. I told him I would get with him, not the other way around. My phone went off again, but this time it was from one of the Hunter sisters, Dali or Devana Okar.

"Hello?" I answered.

"Taria? This is Dali. We have a problem."

"Figures. What's up?" I asked as I moved toward the house.

"We need to hold another meeting. I know the first one was with the five houses' top head members, but we need to find out who is with us and who the hell is against us."

"I agree on that, but where will we hold this, and how does the word get out?" I asked as I walked through the backdoor.

"We haven't had to do this in so many years. I am not sure, but I can ask my elders. It has to be done soon. I know you can feel it getting closer." She was right about that. I could definitely feel something coming at us.

"I may know someone who can make it happen."

"Who? No offense, but this Hunter shit is all new to you. I have been a Hunter for over seventy-four years." Damn, she was that old? They both look good as hell.

"Well, I can ask my father." The silence was on the line when I looked up at my mother's and father's voices entering my room.

"Naki, I understand, but we looked, and he wasn't there. We need to figure something else out because going back there isn't the answer.

We will find him, my pearl." They both looked up at me as I chewed on an apple I got off the large kitchen table. "Taria, is everything ok?" My father asked with concern. Sometimes, looking at him, I still can't believe I had him back in my life. I look so much like him, and I swear his eyes were just as bright as mine are now.

"Yes. I am talking to Dali Okar, and she is asking how we can put out a call for all Hunters so we know who is siding with whom?" I said as the silence stretched on the phone.

"I remember those two well. I also know their family is honorable. I can put out that call just as her mother or father, but mine will reach further."

"I guess you heard him, Dali?" I asked as I finished my apple.

"Yes, yes, I did. Give him my thanks, and please ask him to place the call for the outlands. Thank you again, and I am sure we will see you soon." The call ended before I could ask what the hell was outland.

"She asked if—"

"No need, I heard her. She is very smart to have that idea. Anyone with ill intent cannot cross over to our meeting place."

"Ok, so I take it that you will fill me in on that later, Daddy?" I said, looking between him and my mother.

"Yes. It will take a while. We need to do this because I am going after Beverly soon. She will show her face somewhere, and I will be there to put that bitch in the ground." I now knew the history of my mother and father. It still freaks me the fuck out, but it was knowledge I would need to help me be on my guard and know who my enemies were. Vampires and demons weren't the only things that wanted my life and those closest to me.

"Ok, no problem. I will see my babies and say goodbye to Toya before I set up this damn... dang meeting." I said, trying to fix my cursing before my mother said something. She raised an eyebrow, but my father smiled and pulled her away.

"You do that, baby girl. I will handle that part, and we can review more of the skills you possess as a Cross Hunter at our usual time?" He asked.

"Ahh, I want to say yes, but I am unsure how long this meeting will last."

"We have all the time in the world." I knew damn well he didn't believe that, but what do you tell your daughter. We don't have time because we could all die tomorrow.

"I know, Dad." They turned and went in the other direction, leading them to the downstairs library.

"So, when would you run this meeting with me?" Michael asked. I didn't know how his sneaky old ass creeps up on me like that.

"I hate when you creep. I will talk to you about it before I set up a meeting. I just wanted to see Toya first."

"I guess you forgot about your house guest?" Oh, shit, I did. I completely forgot about Leila's ass.

"No, I didn't. I was giving her time to get herself together." I said, moving closer to him.

"I sent her to your office so she can contact her people. It will be good to establish good relations with her family."

"Her family is cool. I know them already."

"Yes, but not as Elven, you don't. Her mother and father are the leaders of the sect of the Elven races."

"Shit..." Michael reached out, pulling me into him, when I heard the most irritating voice.

"Mike, we need to finish planning where you want to hold the trial and host the elder Blue Bloods?" Camila came into the kitchen with her nose in the air. I couldn't say the vamp wasn't beautiful, but her attitude made her ugly as hell. She looked me over with a quick glance and dismissed me as if I wasn't even there.

"I do need to get back to handling that. Don't make meeting plans without me. Say your goodbyes, and then come to the office." Michael said, ignoring the hoe. She sucked her teeth as she screwed up her face.

"Aight, I got you." I stood on my toes to kiss him, and while I did it, I stared that bitch directly in the eyes.

Masika

My blood burned when I felt that power I hadn't felt in so many years. My son was dead because of my sister's child. A child that should have never been born in the first fucking place. Justin reported to me my sister because she fell for the story to disown my own child. I could never get any information from him about where she was or lived. It was as if whatever spell she cast hid her so well that whoever came in contact with her couldn't, even if they wanted to, tell where it was. It didn't matter what my son tried. He could never say where she was, so I didn't know where to go. Even when he left that place, he still couldn't repeat, write, draw, or do anything that would give up her location. My mind's eye turned toward the west when I felt the first release of her power. My heart broke when I felt my son's life end. He was the only thing I had that was mine. I pushed these thoughts aside as I paced the floor of this large mansion home that belonged to that bitch who helped my sister escape in the first place. I could hear the sound of her heels clicking across the floor.

"Masika! I was under the impression that I would be meeting with your mother, not second best." Beverly snapped. She looked the same as when I saw her all those years ago. She was still a sneaky bitch, but my mother sent me here to take care of Naki's daughter and bring my dear sister to her.

"I don't give a fuck what you thought," I growled. I moved with feline grace, but I had to remember she wasn't just a mere human. "You asked us for help because we had a common goal, and I am here to see it through," I growled in her direction. She moved away quickly and just as gracefully, but her eyes never left mine.

"She interrupted my plans and agreement I had with the Van Allan family," she said with a sneer.

"I guess that runs in her blood. So, what is your proposal?" I asked as I moved back to the floor-to-ceiling windows that covered the house's entire first floor.

"The demon they destroyed that night isn't the only one who wants Taria." I turned because now shit was getting interesting.

"I know of another demon willing to aid us if we also help him. You remember him, don't you? Apu." She said with a smile. I turned swiftly to face her, and I could feel my skin ripple with the need to shift.

"Yesss. He is the one who took my love from me." I hissed.

"Exactly, and he may be the one to give him back to you." She smiled as if she knew she had me. What price will he ask this time? Why would he even offer to bring back my love?

"What's the catch, Beverly?" I asked. I watched as her eyes became calculating, and her smile grew wider.

"We kill that Taria and her entire family."

"That's a given, but what else does he want for his help?" I asked.

"He wants what your mother promised him all those years ago, and if he doesn't get that, your mother's heart will do just fine."

MICHAEL

I moved toward my office, and I could feel Camila behind me, and I knew Malia was already in there. Everyone except Camron was on the property, but I knew my Blade would leave soon. I hated that they thought they had to be by my fucking side at all times. I could handle myself, but I understood that now. Things are different. I still had Winston, Amya, Derrick, Lydia, and these two.

"We need to find a place up to standards that will hold everyone. Since the whole thing with your little Hunter, all eyes are on us. Everyone from the Blue Bloods to the high-ranking turned-vamps questions your relationship with Taria. Also that she has put the supernatural community out in the limelight." Camila said while I sat behind my desk. I had to curve the urge to tell her to get the fuck out.

"Malia, did you buy out the Grand Hotel downtown?" I asked as I stared Camila down. Her eyes widened, and she bowed her head. I heard her suck her teeth because she knew how I felt about how they spoke about Taria. I wouldn't even dignify her with a response. She got that message when she moved across the room to take a call.

"Yes, and there isn't too much that needs to be done to it. We are a go unless you want to change the name or something. I also suggest you have every worker sign a contract and NDAs. Also, hire on some of our own to run the place as well." She looked at her sister and back toward me as she spoke. I could tell she wanted to say something else, but she wisely kept her damn mouth shut.

"I agree with you about those changes. Make it happen, and fast. Also, make sure you hire people I can trust. Make it known that I will read every damn mind whenever I walk into the building, and whatever I find, the consequences will happen swiftly. I want to change the name as well. Change the name to–"

I heard Camila curse under her breath as she ended the call. I wasn't focused on her conversation or the business she had going on because I trusted her to get shit done, but the look of panic and hesitation in her eyes had me leaning back into my chair as my blood boiled.

"What the fuck is the problem, Camila?" I growled. Whatever it was, I knew I would not like the shit.

"There has been a challenge called to have Lily and Garrett removed from the Royal house as your children," she sighed.

Chapter Seven

TARIA

I kissed my God babies again before Toya and Quinn loaded them into the car. The house was quieter, with more than half of the werewolves already gone. Most of the shifters that were left were a few bears, cougars, and a few tigers. I was told that some joined wolf packs or shifters that had no pack of their own came together. It seemed as if Quinn didn't mind what or who was in his pack. That is where his problems were coming from with the Royal werewolf shifters.

"Call me if you need me," I told Toya as I helped her put the twins in the back of the SUV.

"You call me if you need me. I will make a damn portal to wherever you are," Toya said, hugging me. I watched as Rhonda loaded up her parents into another vehicle. I knew Toya had to handle her business, and for all of us to handle what was coming, we had to get our house in order.

"I feel you on that," I said, stepping back.

"Listen, find out what the hell that damn mermaid was talking about. I mean, what the hell else can fucking happen. I mean shit, we defeated Amu and his bitch ass minions, so we can handle whatever the fuck they got going on," Toya said, sucking her teeth. I watched as she looked over the house once more before I answered her.

"First off, I got this, and second you just want to know if there are any mermen down there." I laughed, trying to take the edge off. We all could feel the pressure of some bullshit coming down the road, but it wasn't shit we could do about it until we had answers. Toya burst out laughing before she pulled me down for another hug.

"You're an asshole, Taria, but you're right. I want to know how the hell the procreating is down there. I mean, where the hell do they hide their ding ding?" I rolled my eyes but froze when I felt Michael's anger. Before I could tell Toya to get the hell out of here, the ground shook, and I swore the sky turned a deep shade of red before it was over.

"Aww, shit, who done pissed off King mother fuckin' Kong over here?" Toya said while holding onto the SUV for support.

"Shit! Maybe this isn't the time for us to go, LaToya." Quinn said as he made his way around the truck. His deep brown eyes held the red ring around the irises, and I could see him about to take another form.

"Quinn, Toya, go! It will never be the right time, but you two need to handle your business. I got Michael. Go and be the Alpha you need to be. Toya, go show those Witch hoes who are the biggest Witch bitch." Quinn looked into my eyes for what seemed like forever before he hugged me.

"Aight, sis, just go see what the fuck is going on before he fucks up the warding around the property."

"I got you." I looked at Toya again before turning and starting for the house. I could hear Toya already talking shit.

"My wards are on point! On some real shit, not a damn thing is going—" I tuned her out because I could feel the anger and rage coming from Michael. I don't know what the fuck happened, but I tell you, I hope it was one of those bitches because I could use a good sparring session.

The door opened before I arrived, and I ignored my phone buzzing in my pocket.

"What the hell is going on?" I asked, looking at everyone who was in the room. Derrick was there with his sister. Camila and her sister Malia were also there, along with Marcus, who was by his side. Michael was standing behind his desk, which was crazy as hell because everything else in the room was destroyed. I looked around, but no one answered, so I moved toward Michael. He looked up before I got to him, and his eyes burned like lava. I had seen his second set of fangs before, but it wasn't often. Today they were fully extended, and I knew whatever the hell it was, somebody was about to fucking die. "What happened, Michael? I need someone to fucking answer me, or I will beat the answers out of someone." My eyes flicked toward the sisters, who sneered back at me until the lightning split the sky, and my eyes burned white.

"Sister." I felt a touch on my arm, and I knew it was Marcus, the only one other than Cam who would dare touch me when I was like this.

"Taria. It's cool. It isn't anyone's fault here," Michael said as I watched him struggle to pull his emotions together. It had to be bad to make Michael lose control, even if it was only for a few minutes.

"Ok. Well fucking start talking because the way you look, I feel like we should be preparing for war." I saw the others looking as well and could tell no one else knew what was up. I looked over at the sisters, and when their gaze shifted away, I knew it was going to be something that would make me snap.

"There has been a challenge called to have Lily and Garrett removed from the Royal house as my children." I could feel the wave of anger, but we knew something like this would happen.

"Ok. Ok, maybe I'm not understanding, Michael. We knew it would be some bullshit, so why all this?" I waved my arms around to look at this mess. I heard Derrick growl and Lydia curse. "What?" I asked, looking around. My eyes caught Michael's, and his honey-golden-brown eyes stared into mine. No words were spoken, and I could see the pain and anger he was holding onto.

"Everyone leaves." I was surprised when not a damn word was spoken. My phone went off again, but I didn't even move to check it. "Just fucking answer the thing," Michael growled. My eyes stayed on his as I pulled out the phone. I answered it without looking at who the hell it was.

"I need to call you back."

"We don't have time for that, sweetie. We need to meet and soon." The smooth deep voice was familiar, and not the fucking time for it.

"Didn't I say I would call you and set something up?" I said. I didn't hear the reply because Michael took my fucking phone.

"This is the problem I have, Jason. You believe your government can run shit over here, but that isn't how this will go. We will figure out a time and place where the meeting will take place. If I find out that you or any of your people even think about putting your hands on Taria or any of my people, a war like you have never seen will be at your fucking door. So, sit there and tell your bosses who are listening to wait for the damn call! If you can't, that isn't my problem." Michael disconnected the call without taking his eyes off mine. I reached out, took my phone, and shoved it back into my pocket.

"Talk to me, Michael," I said, but it came out as a whisper.

"I won't let anyone take our children from us, and I will not let anyone Blue Blood or not dictate who I let into my family," Michael said in a low growl.

"I get that, but there is something else you are not saying," I said, stepping closer to him. I could feel his power wrap around my body as his golden eyes looked me over.

"Lily and Garrett are not only shifters but have no direct relation to me. Some can argue since they have no blood relation, they should not carry the Royal title." Michael explained.

"They are our kids Michael! Who the hell can tell us what to do or who our kids can be? No one ever said they are ruling anything." I said, shaking my head. I didn't understand why this was such a big problem or who the hell would care.

"That is true, but they could command our people. They can give orders and demand respect, opening the doors for them to be challenged. Since they have no direct relation to my bloodline and are wolves, Lily and Garrett are seen as threats. Since I am not related to them, the wolf shifters could use them as a claim to the throne and rule over our people." The look on his face showed his disbelief at the words. Hell, Quinn wouldn't do shit like that, but would it be up to him? Thinking along those lines, my blood boiled.

"What! That is bullshit!" I could feel my anger flaring. I pulled it back in, trying to control myself. "Well, first off, Garrett is a part of my blood. Also, LaToya's bloodline, and we know that for a fact. I am your Queen, which makes him a part of our family," I said quieter, so that Michael was the only one who would hear. Not many knew that, and I wanted to keep it that way until I knew who I could trust with our children's lives.

"Yes, and that doesn't need to be known until I find out who exactly is bringing this shit up. We really need to find out more about Lily's parents as well. It doesn't matter what anyone says either way because they are a part of our family, no matter who has a damn problem." I swallowed hard to choke back the words that wanted to fall from my lips. I wanted to say fuck those people or tell them to bring their concerns to me, and I would fix it, but I bit my tongue. I didn't give two shits what these Blue Bloods thought. They will never tell me who is a part of my family.

"I feel you. That is another thing added to the list," I said instead.

"Yeah, but if we figure out who is saying the bullshit, we can handle it and cut it off before it turns into something. I strongly feel this is about something else, and I will figure that shit out. Trust me on that." I licked my lips before taking a deep breath.

"I trust you."

"Good. Now handle what you need to, and let me take care of this. Also, please let Jason know that he calls you anything other than Taria the next time. I will break his fucking neck." Michael said as he turned away. I closed my eyes, praying for answers. I wanted to be here helping with Lily and Garrett's situation, but I also knew Jason had answers to questions about Luke.

"I will pass that along," I said, turning and leaving the destroyed office.

"Taria." I looked back and saw his eyes on me, taking in my every curve.

"Take Leila with you."

"What? Why? It could be dangerous, and I don't want her caught up in our shit."

"I am pretty sure she can handle herself, but it will be good to have another outsider with you — especially one whose clan is known for truth-telling. Having her will benefit us in the long run when we have to make the case to other races about why we allowed knowledge of supernaturals to get loose. Do your thing and just let her watch," he said.

I took in what he was saying because I knew it was right. We may be dealing with our own issues, but the world now knows of all of us, and it was our fault to a certain extent. I didn't think we had to defend why we had no choice, or was it that other supernaturals wouldn't believe our version?

"I got you." I closed the doors behind me and moved to the stairs taking two at a time while dialing Jason.

"Meet me on campus close to the registration building."

"Are you sure that's a good idea?"

"Are you planning to do some sneak shit?"

"No."

"Then meet me in one hour." I disconnected and headed for the room Leila was staying in. Well, no time like the present to see what reactions from people I will get before I return to finish my degree.

MICHAEL

Taria was right about one thing: *Garrett was related to her*. Through her, he is connected to me. Lily was another story, but something told me this went far beyond anyone caring that I took in two shifter children. The only children that could claim the throne will be a child born from Taria. Some other bullshit was going on, and I would damn sure figure it out. I looked at the door before it opened.

"Yes, Camila." I knew she was just relaying the information, but that didn't mean I had to like the shit.

"About the hotel, I know you now have other things on your mind, but I have to finalize everything before–"

"It's fine. Do what you think is best, but I want the hotel's name changed."

"Ok, I can handle that. I already have people lined up. I just will need a name."

"The Lilian-Garrett Grand Suites Hotel," I said. I watched Camila as she opened and closed her mouth.

"Ok. I will make that happen." She turned on her heel and walked out the door. I hope to tell the Blue Bloods that I thought using my children against me would throw me off my game. I stood up as Derrick walked into the office.

"Well, how do you want to handle this?" I could tell that Derrick wanted to say something but was holding back.

"How about you tell me what you're thinking." A smile pulled at his lips before he answered.

"I don't think the Van Allan family is the only one who wants your crown."

"What does it matter because I have the power of Gio now. No one can take that away."

"That is true, but it can be given away."

"Why the hell would I do something like that?" I growled. I leaned over to lace up my Nikes.

"What father do you know that wouldn't do anything for their children?" I looked up with a furrow in my brows.

"You think this time, one of the families will come to my kids to get to me?"

"That's what I would do." I studied Derrick, and I could see clearly in his green eyes; he was dead serious.

"Who do you think it is? I had suspicions, and my power was vast, but I didn't know all." The only thing that hasn't changed is that I still couldn't see anything about those closest to me.

"Patrick Parks." I looked toward him sharply because that was the last name I would have suspected to leave his lips.

"Your grandfather?" I questioned.

"Yes, because he called to order me to keep an eye on the two children. I don't know why or what he wants, but he seemed very interested in who or what Lily is." I could see how tense his body became while he spoke. He was prepared to take whatever I did to him without fighting back.

"What about Lydia?" His eyes snapped to mine.

"She doesn't have anything to with–"

"She has always been his favorite Derrick. We both know this to be a fact."

"Let me talk to her, Michael." I could see the panic in his eyes. What his grandfather asked him to do could get him killed or worse.

"You have twenty-four hours to give me answers as to why the fuck your family wants my daughter. What does Patrick know that we don't?" I could feel my words were laced with a command and a threat. If Derrick didn't get me the needed answers, I would tear his family apart, including his sister. I didn't want to because he and she were part of my circle, but plans against my own will never be tolerated, no matter who the hell they were.

"Yes, my King."

Chapter Eight

TARIA

"This is WJBT 97.2 Hot Jamz Baltimore, and I am your host, DJ Tracks! Let's talk about the hot topic over these past months. Do you believe in the supernatural, or is this just fake news? Phone lines are open, people!"

"I don't know if that s**t was real, but we all know the government is hidin' s**t all the time!"

"Thanks, man, next caller, you on."

"Hey, this is Kesha. Yeah, so I believe that was real! My grandma passed out on the floor. I swear she died that night, and she sat up in tears when it was over! She said God was real!"

"Wow! I am glad she ok, Kesha. God Bless. Ok, next caller, talk to me. What do you believe?"

"Yeah, what's good, Tracks?"

"Nothing, man. Tell me what you think?"

"I don't know. I mean, all that could have been staged. I mean, they always tryna keep our attention away from the real problems we got going on in the world."

"Ok, ok, what about that interview, though?"

"I mean, she could have been a part of it as well. We don't know anything for sure. I need to see it myself in person."

"Ok, thanks. Next caller, you on!"

"Hey, Tracks! Shout out to MSU! This Stacey repping for all the journalism students."

"Aight Morrison State College on the mic. So, tell me, Ms. Stacey, what do you think?"

"Well, I have seen that girl around campus and in class. She is a real person, but I never saw anything unusual about her, but I don't think she is a lair. Hell, all those murders happening on and off-campus, something is going on."

"So, wait, you know her?"

"I mean, I don't know her, but I do know she used to work for the school paper. From what I heard, she hadn't been seen lately."

"Aight, Ma! Stay in school, and be careful. Ok, y'all, one more call. Next caller, tell me what you think?"

"If this is all real and what we saw really happened, then we have much more to worry about. How do we know if they won't attack us, humans, next? I mean, they stopped what we think is a demon, but how do we know if that is true?"

"Say less, fam. I feel you on that."

"Another thing that has me thinking is what the hell else is out there. I mean, we are talkin demons, vampires, werewolves, and, I guess, people that can throw stuff from their hands! What's next? Big Foot, swamp thing, aliens, or whatever. Hell, I want to know who will protect us from them!"

"Aight, thanks, my man, but that's it for now—a lot of questions and not enough answers. I will say this. I believe it, and if that thick sister with the fangs wants to do another interview, holla at me. Ok, that's all the time we have. I'm out!"

I cut the radio off with a shake of my head. Maybe showing up on campus wasn't such a great idea, but perhaps it will show others I mean no threat. I took a deep breath pushing it aside for now because I wanted to know more about Leila.

I side-eyed Leila as I drove toward Morrison State University to meet up with Jason. She hadn't said much since we left the house but was engrossed in her phone. It was crazy because looking at her now, I would have never known what she truly was if I had never fallen down that paranormal rabbit hole. I had known her for a few years, and she never let on that she was different at all.

"Why are you looking at me like I am an alien or something?" Leila asked, putting her phone away. She smiled, and her even straight teeth flashed at me.

"What the hell happened to the sharp fangs that were in your mouth earlier?" I asked as I looked from her and back to the road. I switched lanes in my new car that Michael insisted I had to have. I wouldn't front, though, because this shit was hot. I loved my black-on-black Dodge Challenger Hell Cat.

"Oh, my God," she laughed as she shook her head. For a split second, I could see her markings before they disappeared again.

"What?"

"Girl, you are crazy. You know I can't walk around like that. Do you walk around with fangs out?"

"You have a point," I said, smiling. "How bad do you think it is with other species?" I asked in all seriousness. I wanted to know who I needed to talk to so that I could repair the damage Peter and Victor caused trying to take over the damn world.

"You have a lot of different supernaturals already on your side Taria. I walked around your home for a bit, and it isn't just vampires or even wolves. You have a whole damn community. I just have a question I hope you will answer."

"What? I will answer if I can," I said, getting off at the exit.

"Why did you hide? I mean, you are a Hunter, and I thought a Cross Hunter was all about protecting? We meaning all supernaturals, have been targets from some evil ass shit lately." It was like a slap in the face, but at the same time, I knew nothing about the supernatural world. I felt it deep in my soul because I knew what my role was supposed to be in this world, and if my parents hadn't kept it from me, maybe I could have done something.

"I wasn't hiding," I said with a sigh.

"I have known you for a few years, Taria, and you have never given off this type of power. I don't know how all this vampire business came into play, but you are a Hunter, and they give off an energy that can't be explained. We know to keep our distance but also that you keep the real shit that goes bump at bay at night." She finished with a wave out the window as if demons were running the streets or something. I sighed because she thought I had kept this hidden from her, and she felt like a fool for not figuring it out.

"I had no idea who or what my father was or is. I knew nothing until I took one innocent vacation with Toya to Florida, and everything changed." I hit the wheel but rubbed it after for hurting my baby.

"Ha! You were crazy thinking going anywhere with Toya's crazy ass was innocent!" She laughed. I smiled, but it was true. I knew absolutely nothing at the start of this.

"You may be right about that, but I knew nothing. This is all new to me, Leila." I said, gesturing to her. I stopped at a red light and turned to look at her.

"I believe you, Taria. It's just I can't believe this. My clan has been searching for the original Hunter family. We have been looking for a member of the Cross family for well over one hundred years."

"Why?" I asked as a horn blew. I turned back to the road and pressed the gas. We weren't far from the school, so I looked for parking. Looking around, I knew I had to go back and finish. I miss being here, and I miss working on the paper.

"You don't already know? I mean, you stopped the first demon who was trying to come through, but that isn't the only one."

"Yeah, believe me, I know." I rolled my eyes but saw when a car pulled out of a spot. I pressed on the gas and backed in.

"Thank God! That will make things easy when I bring my parents, our clan leaders, to meet you."

"Wait. What?"

"Yes, they need to give you the other books that have been lost. You are the only family that should be able to read them."

"What books?" Leila was dropping shit on me like I knew what she was talking about. I thought I had all the books from my family.

"Jaser, entrust my people with books that belonged to your family. You really don't know what I am talking about, do you?"

"No, I don't," I said, turning the car off. I turned to face her in my seat and saw the marking flare to life on her skin.

"It was told to me long ago that the son of Jaser disappeared before he could give him what he would need when the time comes. He didn't fully trust the other Hunter families with this information," she said in a thick accent. It was weird because I couldn't place where it was from, nor had I ever heard her speak this way before.

"Why would he trust your people with something so important?" I could feel the Impundulu shifting inside my mind as it woke from a long sleep.

"Because my clan was there when the heavens sang, and Jaser was blessed with the gift of becoming the first of these world protectors." Silence filled the car for so long that I jumped at my phone buzzing.

"I need to speak with my father before meeting your people," I said while digging into my pocket for the phone.

"I thought your father was dead?"

"So did I, but–" I let the sentence linger as I read the message. Jason was already here, and apparently, so were the news stations. "What the hell is he trying to pull?" I growled. I closed my eyes and took in a deep calming breath. I hit the call button, and it was answered right away.

"Taria?"

"Yes."

"I just wanted to give you a heads up. I felt you might not even know what was going down."

"Thank you, Henry."

"Always. The Sun will always have your back." I ended the call and looked over toward Leila. "Do you have permission to come out, or are you going to glamour or something?"

"Pros to you for even knowing that word."

"Seriously. The news stations are here, and I don't know what the hell the alphabet boys got up their sleeves.

"I am going to remain undercover. That will give me the best advantage in getting information. This is what we do. We watch and report the truth. Everyone knows an Elven from the Moon Clan is the recorder of history. What we witness is always told in truth."

"Ok, bet. Well, get ready for the bullshit." I exited the car and sent a quick text informing Michael about the camera crew.

Chapter Nine

TARIA

Leila went ahead of me so we wouldn't be seen coming together. That was fine with me 'cause if shit broke out, I wouldn't have to worry about her getting caught up with my mess. The storm grew in my mind, and a voice I hadn't heard since I almost died spoke to me.

"Taria. Do not let your guard down. My power may protect you from many things, but not everything. Family can be your worst enemy."

The lightning and rain and my mind crashed around as if it was going to break free and wreak havoc. I could feel the Impundulu settle back down in my mind, and I didn't think I needed to respond. I got the message, and I ultimately agreed with it. The problem was, why did it feel the need to warn me now? What would happen, and who was it that it had the almighty Impundulu on edge? I saw Jason leaning against the wall of the admissions building. I could see the reporters. They were focused on the play that was going on outside of the Art

Institute. I could tell they really weren't paying attention because they were tipped off, but why. What game was Jason playing?

"Hey, sexy. Thank you for coming. My bosses have questions, and they want me to get them." He said with a smile. A dimple popped on his right cheek with his sexy smirk. I smiled as his eyes roamed me up and down, but I didn't say anything.

"It's no problem, but I think you should quit with the nicknames," I said with a raised eyebrow.

"Why? Is the vamp on some shit? He mad 'cause he got competition or something?" I didn't even reply. I shook my head at him.

"What's going on, Jason? What do you know about Luke Van Allan? Where is he?"

"That is the question I am here to ask you. He is missing, and there are dead agents everywhere. I don't know any human people who could have gotten to him."

"So, you thought you would accuse me?" I asked, laughing at the bullshit. I bit my lip, trying to keep the convo low-key. As a few students passed us, I caught some double takes, but no one stopped.

"Who else would it be? I don't think you had anything to do with it, but come on. Who in the hell could have done this?"

"Naw. Why did you have him in the first place?" My voice hardened. I was trying not to let it come out as a command. I wouldn't say I like to play with other people's minds. I could feel Leila wasn't too far away, and I knew she could hear every word.

"We were trying to help him," Jason said. I could tell he didn't even believe that lie.

"Bullshit!" Something wasn't right, and Jason was in the middle of it.

"Listen, I don't run shit. I didn't think it was right to take him, but he was hurt. I said to turn him over to you and your people. That would, at the most, gain the department goodwill. I don't make the decisions, Taria. I do my damn job."

"Even at the risk of killing everyone, you swore to protect?"

"What?"

"From my understanding, your people, the organization you run with, low-key made a deal long ago never to imprison our kind. That is a breach of the deal."

"Your kind? Taria, you were just as human as I am not long ago. What are they having you believe?" He looked sick.

"From my understanding, Jason, what do your bosses have you believing?"

"That's enough, Jason. We can take it from here." I turned to a new voice. This wasn't the man that was at the interview but someone new.

"Sir. I got this. Taria was just about to tell me who could have killed our men."

"You can't be this dumb," I said, looking back to Jason.

"Listen, just don't react to him. He wants to cause a scene," Jason said openly. I looked at him, trying to figure out how he knew to do that.

"Agent Davis, stand down!" The dude had no reason to get all loud.

"Sir!" This would play out, but if they thought they could take me, they all were tripping.

"How can I help you, Mr–"

"Agent Hood. Agent Jack Hood and you are Taria Cross, one of the monsters that killed my men." I heard the collective gasps and the reporters zooming in on the conversation. I just didn't know what purpose he was creating this scene for. I cut my eyes to Jason, seeing the apparent anger and confusion. He stepped forward and held out an arm to push me back.

"Sir, you asked me to learn some things from Mrs. Cross. Why are you making a spectacle of this?"

"Agent, you were to bring her in for questioning in the murders of ten Federal Agents. She and her friends are the only "THINGS" we know of that could have done what was done to our agents. To all human men and women, we are looking out for all of our best interests." I held back the storm brewing inside me. Seeing the snipers, they had in place, all the cameras pointed our way. I looked around. They wanted a battle, and I damn sure wanted to give them one. I looked down as Jason pushed me further behind him. That would not work, but I will take note that he was trying to protect me. I moved fast, stepping around Jason. I stood in front of him and didn't make any sudden movements or flash any fangs. I knew I had got my point across. Agent Hood took a step back but recovered quickly. He stood tall at 6'6", with a slight muscle build and dark brown hair cut close to his scalp.

"Mr. Hood, I agreed to meet Agent Davis here to speak with him about one of my people who went missing during the attack my people saved this world from. We did not know that the government captured and held him prisoner. Is that what happened, or am I mistaken about that?" I could hear the whispers and murmurs of the students and reporters who were waiting for what he had to say.

"We did no such thing, and I do not appreciate you deflecting what your people have done to our men!"

"I am not deflecting anything. Before yesterday I had no idea that one of ours was missing or, should I say, taken against his will. Not to mention that the boy you took is a minor, and his parents want to know where he is. Do you have those answers?"

"If it wasn't you who took him from our care after you and your people left that poor child to die, then who would it be?" He asked. That was a good question, but I felt we would not like the answer.

"That I couldn't tell you, but we will find him and find out what happened. If he is harmed, you will have to answer to that."

"Is that a threat?" He asked, raising his voice. I smiled and shook my head.

"No. You should ask someone with a higher clearance than you, sir. If what I think happened has gone down, I am not the one you should be afraid of." I looked around as everything felt like moving in slow motion. I could feel the portal opening, but I wasn't sure what was coming out. My hand was behind my back when a black opening formed right behind Agent Hood, and the face of Masika smiled at me.

"NO!" I screamed as the entire campus erupted into chaos.

Michael

Looking at my phone, I knew shit was starting. "Shit," I growled as I stood up from my desk. The room was somewhat put back together, but I would have to replace some things.

"Daddy, that is not a nice word." I looked down at Lily as she sat at her desk. I had to make one because she sometimes wouldn't leave my office.

"My bad, Lily." I smiled, but she didn't see it. She was so engrossed in the picture she was drawing. "I will be right back. I need to make a call." I started for the door when I heard her say the colored pencil down.

"Everything will work out just fine, Daddy. No one can keep us apart. You, me, Mommy, and Garrett have always belonged together." I turned around slowly to look at my princess. She had already picked up her pencil and started drawing once again. I had no idea what the hell to say to that. "I love rainbows," she smiled at the picture. I was about to ask her more when my phone rang, and I saw it was Malia. I turned for the door again.

"What now?" I asked as I made my way to my mother's room. I know she asked for time, but I needed her. She knew how to talk to these stuck-up Blue Blood bitches. I wasn't in the mood, and they would be here soon.

"I contacted Dax as you asked, and he said little about Lily's parents were known. They came to him right before their little war broke out, and they died."

"Fuck! Ok, did he have anything else to say?" I asked as I stepped outside my mother's door.

"Just that she had some things belonging to her parents that were sent over once you officially adopted them. Maybe something is in them that will help in finding out more."

"Aight. Thank you for looking into that. Help your sister get my hotel together before your parents and everyone else arrives."

"At least it will just be the first five families of Blue Bloods."

"Yeah, for now, at least. The others will follow in due time," I said as the door opened in front of me.

"Michael, I... I may not like your Queen, but I will do everything to ensure yours and her crowing go right. You are the King, and I will follow your lead." The call ended. I stared into my mother's eyes and felt the relief all over again that I had her back in my life before we could truly enjoy that we had to get our house in order.

"What do you need, Michael? I am here to help you," she said, touching my face. She already looked much better than she did just a few hours ago.

"I think someone of Blue Blood wants to harm my children. More specifically, Lily." I could feel my fangs wanting to burst loose, but I had to keep control. I didn't have full control over all my powers just yet, and I didn't wasn't to hurt anyone.

"What? Who would want... ok, what do you need from me? I will never let anyone harm my grandchildren." I watched as my mother's eyes glowed almost white.

"I need you to find out who her parents were. I need to know why anyone would want her and what they would try to use her for." I said.

"Yes. I can do that. Where should I start?"

"How about starting with meeting your grandchildren and taking it from there?" I could see her spine stiffening and my mother returning to herself.

"Go and handle what you need to and leave this to me. Nothing will happen to our family, not again. Not while I still breathe, and the sun still shines." She moved by me with fluid grace as she moved down the hall, reclaiming her life one step at a time.

I pulled up to the hotel and saw Camila and Malia had everything under control. Before tonight, I hoped the name would be in place before the Blue Bloods arrived. I could sense someone or something watching me, but I didn't give away that I noticed it. I stepped through the main doors and looked around. Everything from the floors to the front desks was way over the top. The white marble floors gleamed in the lighting, and the white gold trimming that lined the walls had me shaking my head.

"You know as well as I do that they expect this type of luxury," Camila said. Her long legs caught up to my quick pace as I looked around.

"That they do. Will the grand ballroom be ready in time for the crowning ceremony?" I asked when I felt intense anger and fear hit my chest. I stopped in my tracks, knowing full well it was Taria and something had gone wrong.

"What is it?" Camila asked. She looked around, determining if something was wrong or out of place. I didn't answer as I focused on Taria. The panic receded, but she wasn't answering my mental call to her. I wasn't feelin' the shit, and that alone had me turning on my heel.

"Michael! We have shit we need to handle. You have to approve—"

"I don't have time," I growled. I pulled out my phone and dialed Taria's number when the screen lit up with Marcus's call.

"What?" I snapped. I didn't have time for more questions or fucking guidance on love and shit.

"My parents will be here within the hour. I just found out a few minutes ago, and they have asked to stay at your home." He said without preamble. I felt a soft touch on my mind, and the smell of Taria invaded my senses.

"It's bullshit going on, but I am handling it. We must unite our people to start talking with humans at the top. We don't have the time to be playing politics at every turn. Please do what you must, and don't worry about me. I got this."

I stopped in my tracks as her voice faded from my mind. I didn't answer her, but if she thought I would not show up, she was fucking crazy. I just had to get this shit done to go to my *Kindred Soul*.

"They want to see my mother," I stated.

"My father is her brother Michael, but I understand if you do not want them at your home." I knew he understood my origin, but this would benefit my mother.

"What are their thoughts about Taria?" I asked. Family or not, if they do not accept my Queen, then they will not sit at my table. Marcus wasn't stupid, and he would know how I felt in that regard.

"Mother is unsure but not hostile. You know your uncle, Michael; I don't think you will have a problem with my father. I think my mother needs a chance just as I did."

"When are you leaving?" I asked instead of agreeing.

"I am pulling up to Shannara's home as we speak. Will you let them in, Michael?"

"Yes," I said and disconnected.

"Camila, everything looks to be in place, but I want security to be bumped up. Speak to Dax Rayne and his brothers about that, and also make sure these vamps and other sups are vetted properly. I know this is all a rush job, and things will not be perfect, but I want to know there are no damn snakes in The Lilian-Garrett. Do you get me on that? I will hold you personally responsible for any and all fuck-ups."

"Yes, I understand, and it will be done." I nodded at her and walked out of the doors. Toya was gone, and I needed someone to lay some wards around this place. Witches were strong in warding, but so were Hunters. I jumped behind the wheel of my SUV and pulled off. I had a feeling something other than government assholes would go down. As I turned, I hit downtown traffic, which allowed me to hit the steering wheel's call button.

"Michael, is everything ok, son?" His calling would be funny if I didn't know how old he was. He wasn't fully human, and just how he said it reminded me of my father and that I would never hear him say that again.

"Shit," I growled.

"Michael? What the hell is going on? Where is Taria?" I realized I wasn't saying anything and had to get my mind back into the game.

"I am on my way to Taria as we speak, but that isn't why I was calling."

"Ok, then tell me what's up?" I could hear a whisper of someone in the background, and it sounded like chanting.

"Are you busy?"

"Yes and no. I am working on something for Taria, but I'm good. You can talk to me."

"Aight. Are you any good at warding a property? I just need something to know who or what can enter."

"Didn't you already have LaToya Grey and her mother ward your land?"

"Yes, but I just purchased a hotel because the Blue Bloods will be coming into town," I said as I moved to the left lane.

"I see. Yes, I can ward it for you. Just text me the address, and I will go and handle that in a few. Also, to beef that up too, you and my daughter should also line the hotel area with your blood. That will give it another layer of protection because Taria and LaToya are connected."

"I got you. We will do that as well. Thank you, Joziah."

"Anytime, son. Now please get to my daughter because Garrett just entered and is frantic. Something is going to happen." The call dropped, and I pulled over.

"Fuck this!" I jumped out of the truck, which was barely in park. The traffic was thick, but I would move faster if I were on foot. I reached out for Taria again, but all I felt was a large black hole where my heart should have been.

Chapter Ten

KATHERINE

I knew it was time and would do anything for my son and now my grandchildren. I stood in Michael's office doorway and watched Lily talk to Garrett about everything under the sun.

"Daddy is afraid someone will take us. I told him that's crazy," Lily said with her small arms in the air.

"Lily, you don't know what is going on, ok. Don't worry, Mom and Dad will figure everything out, and then we can actually do family stuff." Garrett said. He sat facing the window on the large couch, reading a book that looked too big for his small hands.

"Yeah, we need to do it now before you leave and go away to school."

"What are you talking about?" Garrett asked. He closed the book and looked at the pretty little girl. Her smooth baby skin and high cheekbones told me my son would be in trouble. Her eyes caught my attention because they reminded me of Jessiah's eyes. The pain of his loss never left me, and I knew I was projecting.

"Garrett, look! It's Bibi!" She pointed at me. I saw Garrett turning around and rolling his eyes.

"Lilian, have you ever asked her if you can call her…" He saw that I was standing there, and he stood up quickly. "Lily, come here, please." He said it so quietly, but she heard him and hurried to his side. She grabbed his open hand as they both stared at me.

"That is a very pretty name, Lilian," I said with a smile. Garrett cleared his throat but held Lily's hand tightly.

"Ahh, can we do something for you… your majesty… or ma'am… I mean…" He stuttered nervously. I moved to make my way into the room, hating myself for not meeting them sooner.

"No, no, Garrett, you call me Grandma or Bibi. Whatever you two want to call me is fine with me. You don't have to be nervous; we are all family." I smiled as I stood back up. "I am sorry it has taken me so long to meet my two grandchildren formally, but–" I smiled, holding out my arms for them both. It didn't take Lily long to launch herself into my arms, and I felt a peace I hadn't felt in a century come over me. I hugged her tightly and watched as Garrett smiled.

"I'm sorry if I bothered you at night," Garrett said as I sat Lily on her feet. I breathed in as I spoke, and a familiar scent filled my nose. I blinked rapidly because it had to be. She was just so close to Michael all the time. She smelled just like us but different.

"Bibi?" I looked down to see Lily watching me.

"Sorry. You never bothered me, Garrett. You actually gave me a reason to get myself moving," I said, taking Lily's hand. "Now, I want to know everything about you, and leave nothing out," I smiled as we all sat on the couch, and Lily began talking.

"Well… I was born and had a sister, but she didn't make it–"

Taria

I saw the flame forming in her hands, and I moved. My hand was already on the hilt of my short sword, so I pulled it free. I pushed Jason hard, sending him flying backward. I heard his body hit the doors, making them crash in when I reached out for dumbass Agent Hood. I saw his steel-gray eyes widen and an almost smile form on his lips because he thought I was attacking him. "Move, you idiot!" I screamed while jumping, touching his shoulder so lightly I didn't even think he noticed until he flew through the air. I pushed him into his fellow agents, knocking them all down just in time as the fire missed them but burned the hell out of my right shoulder.

I didn't acknowledge the pain because I didn't have time. Masika stepped through the portal, along with at least ten large sleek panthers and fucking Condemned humans. The screams and loud roars brought my attention back into focus as my blade met with my aunt's.

"I told you, girl, I would be back!" I moved fast, sweeping her legs from under her as I threw my sword at a Condemned, trying to claw at a student. I bit my lip hard while leaning over, pulling the ugly thing off the girl. I pulled my sword from its back and kicked it in the chest. I then used my nails and dug into my palms to coat the blade with my blood. I could feel another Condemned coming up behind me, but I spun around and stabbed the thing in the face. As blood flowed from my mouth, I wiped it over my arms and face. This was something my father taught me to do. Just letting them touch my blood could put them down enough. I could take them out. I heard shots to my left —pop, pop, and screaming as people ran from the panthers and zombies. I moved from zombie to zombie, helping out whoever I could in the process.

"Taria!" A rough female voice shouted over the screaming. I turned and saw that Masika was holding Jason by the throat. Her clawed hands squeezed as his hand clawed at hers.

"Nothing you or your family can do to stop us from taking this world. You will pay for taking my son's life! Your mother will feel the pain I felt to lose a child." Her eyes glowed brightly as her face shifted. I cut through whatever got in my way as I pushed forward to save Jason. I pushed humans toward the buildings' safety, but I could save everyone, and that is what they wanted.

"I'm right fucking here!" I screamed as the wind blew and lightning split the sky. I could still feel the burn of the fire, and it felt like it was eating my skin, but I pushed that aside. A panther leaped at me, but I caught it by the throat and spun as I slammed the panther into the ground and used my sword, stabbing it in the heart.

"Yes! But what would be fun if your friends didn't suffer first? You can't save them all!" I felt panic take over as I tried to control my emotions. Too many innocent people were around, and I couldn't predict the lightning strikes would hurt someone. I kicked, punched, and sidestepped as I moved closer to this crazy-ass bitch. I saw her watching me, and her jaw was almost completely unhinged as she opened it wider to bite Jason's head off.

"You want me! Drop him!" I screamed. I moved faster, but every zombie and every panther came at me as if it was planned. Before they all filled my vision, I saw her lean over Jason before I felt teeth and claw tearing at my chest.

Jason

I didn't even see Taria move until I went flying and hit the ground hard as fuck. The breath knocked me out, but I knew I had to move. If she attacked Hood, all hell would break loose. When I pulled myself up and got my gun out, I knew hell was already here. I saw Taria move Hood out of the way before being attacked by a woman who looked more animal than human.

Along with her came the things I prayed for. I would never see those things again. Along with that huge ass, panthers streamed through what I guessed was a portal. I jumped to my feet as I fought through the burn in my chest and moved.

"Everyone get out of the way! Get inside!" I screamed as I pushed people toward the buildings. I didn't know if that would save them, but I had to try. I took two shots at one of those things, but it kept coming. I shot the stomach, leg, and chest, but nothing stopped the thing from coming for me. "Shit!" I said when the grotesque-looking thing almost had me. It fell to the ground as small thin pale white blades slammed into its temple. I didn't waste time because I didn't know if it was down for good or not. I looked to my left, seeing the girl that was with Taria last night, moving swiftly with ease through the mass of people taking out panthers and whatever those things were. She caught my eyes before disappearing and ended up beside the agents, helping them by watching their backs. I shook my head and moved again, shooting whatever came at me that looked like a threat. I saw Taria moving so fast I could have told you it was more than one of her. I tried to get to her and help her however I could. Hell, at least, watches her back.

I didn't know who these sups were, but this is what my team was supposed to be for not starting trouble with the people willing to help us. "Taria!" I yelled while ducking under a panther that leaped at me. I looked behind me but saw another white blade lodged in its heart. I kept moving forward when I saw the woman who almost killed Agent Hood circle behind the panthers and the other things. She was going to attack Taria, but I wouldn't let that shit go down. I jumped over students' bodies but couldn't tell if they were dead or alive. The chaos was massive, and I swear I saw a few cameramen and camerawomen still fucking filming.

I was close when I let off three more shots into a panther that almost had me by the leg when I noticed it was my last magazine. It didn't matter because I could let the bitch get to Taria before I could warn her. I was almost to her, and I let my tactical knife slip into my palm as I moved behind the woman. Before I was ten feet away, she vanished before my eyes, but then I felt clawed hands wrap around my throat.

"Taria!" The woman's rough voice shouted over all the screaming and moaning. I saw her turn to see me. Her eyes shone bright, and I thought I could see lightning flashing in them. Even with her covered in blood, she was sexy as hell, and I could see the fear and anger playing across her face as she looked my situation over. Her clawed hands squeezed my throat, and I could feel her nails' sharp tips pierce my skin. I didn't care if she killed me as long as Taria got away. She saved what was left of my family, so it felt right I repay that debt. The woman laughed as Taria pushed forward to get to us.

"Nothing you or your family can do to stop us from taking this world. You will pay for taking my son's life! Your mother will feel the pain I felt to lose a child." My vision was fading, but the woman's eyes glowed brightly, and her fucking face shifted and changed. Her mouth widened as her teeth became long, sharp daggers I knew I would never walk away from.

"I'm right fucking here!" I heard Taria scream. I felt the wind blow, and lightning saw lightning split the sky. I knew this would be the end for me, but I refused to go out without fighting. I still held my knife in my hand, but it was hard to lift my arm up. My life was draining out of me as I slowly suffocated to death. I didn't know if that was better to go out that way or to have this creature bite my fucking head off. At least that might end this pain quicker, but I would give Taria all the help she needs. The woman turned back to Taria with the most grotesque smile.

"Yes! But what would be fun if your friends didn't suffer first? You can't save them all!" I saw Taria kicking, punching, and sidestepping as she tried moving closer. The woman turned back to me, and I saw her jaw almost completely unhinged as she opened it wider to bite my head off.

"You want me! Drop him!" Taria screamed, and I knew now was the time I should be fighting. The blackness in my vision was taking over, and I had no more time. Taria wouldn't make it, but at least she tried. I raised my arm, but she caught it with her other hand. Her claws dug into my wrist, making it impossible for me to hold on to the knife. A silent scream tore out of my throat as she snapped my wrist. I could see the blood and her face coming closer to my own. I couldn't see Taria anymore, but I heard her screams, and I hated being so fucking weak I couldn't save myself. Before my vision failed, I saw two thin white blades land on the side of the woman's neck, making her cry out in pain. I knew it wouldn't be enough to save me this time because she turned back with burning blood-red eyes and pulled mine to her open mouth.

"Too bad I must kill you because you would make a great panther for my army. Still, I am sure you will be DELICIOUS!"

MASIKA

Things were going better than I thought as the Condemned and the panthers swarmed Taria. I didn't think I would get this lucky and find a friend out of her protection this quickly. It was too bad that I would eat him. He could turn into a panther with his injuries. His scent and blood were strong, but I needed Taria to feel the pain of loss, and he would be the first. I brought him closer when I felt two sharp pricks of pain and a burning sensation. I didn't have long before that Elven magic sank into my blood. I had to dig it out, and soon. I shook off the pain and focused on the male, who looked back at me with hatred and brought him closer to my fangs.

"Too bad I must kill you because you would make a great panther for my army. Still, I am sure you will be DELICIOUS!" I hissed when I saw a bright flash of light fill my vision. I dropped the man letting him fall to the ground as energy blast after blast slammed into my chest. I roared in pain and shifted.

"Naw, bitch!" I was mid-shift when I saw the King of Vampires approaching me. He lifted two guns, but I knew that wouldn't harm me. I was way too powerful for all that shit. When he smiled, that is what caught me by surprise. His guns glowed a deep orange as he poured his energy into them. The Elven poison was making it harder to shift, and I would not make it. I watched as he sent bullet after bullet in my direction when I felt different energy behind me. A portal was opening, and I felt hands on my body, pulling me back but not before two more of his shots slammed into my body.

"You must make a new deal to heal this body." I couldn't see, but the hissing speech told me what held me in its arms.

"To kill those bitches, I will make whatever deal is necessary," I whispered.

"My master will make you whole." Those were the last words I heard before everything faded to black.

Chapter Eleven

MICHAEL

I had to remove my shots and make them count because I could feel the portal opening. I saw the Druid reaching out for that bitch Masika, but she wasn't getting off that easy. I threw power blast after blast in all directions, hitting zombies and panthers alike. I could feel Taria, and I knew she was in trouble. Masika dropped Jason, and I commended him for his bravery because he thought of trying to save Taria. He knew what she did for his brother. If he died giving her more time, he would gladly do it.

As the Druid pulled Masika into the portal, I pulled out my Glocks and pushed my energy into them, making each bullet just as powerful as a grenade hitting you directly. I knew not all hit her, but I know for damn sure some of them did. I couldn't release my full power because there were too many humans, and they could die being so close. I reached Jason as my eyes scanned for Taria. She was still alive but in pain. I knew she would want me to save everyone else before I came for her, but fuck that.

"Save her..." Jason coughed. I looked at him, overseeing the damage inside and out. I lifted my wrist to my mouth and bit down. "What the hell are you—" I didn't let him finish. I let a few drops enter his mouth, then laid my hand over his chest. I could feel his body going through the change. He didn't know it yet, but his world was about to shift into one he had never known.

"My Queen doesn't need saving. She just needs someone at her back." I felt the presence at my back. I turned and let off four more shots, stopping two panthers and a zombie and their tracks. Leila was ducking before me as if I was aiming at her.

"Leila, take care of him. He is becoming," I growled.

"Yes, I got him," she said as I turned around.

I saw the pile that covered Taria and headed for it. I used my telekinetic abilities to move people out of the way to push them indoors. I also used my power to stop wounds from bleeding, saving some more time. As I made my way to Taria, I could tell that some wouldn't make it if we didn't end this shit now. A flash of white-hot lightning split the air as the wind picked back up. I knew they would hurt someone if I didn't move these people out of the way. I saw some agents shooting at the pile covering Taria. The lightning was getting closer, and the next blast would throw them off their feet if they didn't move. I ran into the middle of the group, who started yelling, but I held up my hands.

"Quiet!" I caught each eye of the agents. I saw the one giving Taria problems, and I moved to him. My powers were being stretched more than ever, but I wasn't about to disappoint her. These people may or may not believe we are not the enemy, but we would save them, anyway. I could see the hate and disgust over his features, but I ignored it. I knew my eyes burned gold, and my fangs reached my chin. "When I let you go, give your people the order to run and hide. If you do not, you all will die." I released my hold on the agents but didn't stay to see if they took my words to heart. The wind was whipping around, and I moved and blocked whoever I could when the white light filled the campus. Everything was quiet as I shielded two reporters behind a bench.

"CLOSE YOUR EYES!" I screamed out the mental call and prayed everyone listened.

KATHERINE

Lily talked a mile a minute, but I loved every minute of it. Garrett didn't seem to mind, but I caught him rolling his eyes occasionally as Lily told me how she first shifted. I was about to ask her a question when Garrett jumped up.

"What is it, Garrett?" I asked, looking at his face. His eyes were enormous, but his hands were in little fists.

"Why would a family member attack their own family? It makes no sense." He shook his head and looked toward the windows.

"Sometimes, baby, a family member can be your worst enemy. I can tell you one thing, though." I said. He turned back to look me in the eyes.

"What?" I could hear the small growl in his voice just as I could feel the battle going on. My blood was fighting. For some reason, Garrett also knew what was happening.

"Your parents can handle it. The family that they are building together will be strong, and they will never attack each other. They will fight beside one another." I held his eyes until he nodded.

"I'm going to my room to finish reading." I wanted to stop him, but I knew the only thing to help him would be when his parents returned.

"Ok, but just remember they will always come back for you," I said as he walked to the door.

"I know, Bibi. Just like you came back for us." Garrett said nothing else as he walked out and closed the door. I looked back down at Lily, and her familiar eyes stared back. I knew she was young, but the wisdom in her eyes made me take a breath.

"Garrett will understand Bibi soon. They will always return to us, even if they have to fight death itself." I opened my mouth to say something to this little girl, but she smiled. "I also have books and pictures. That's all I have left of my old mom and dad, but that's ok. Do you want to see them?" I was so taken aback by this girl I just nodded yes. I stood up, and she reached out, took my hand, and headed out of the office.

We entered her room, and she dropped my hand to run over to a large wooden chest.

"This was my mommy's chest, but Taria said it's mine now, and I can put special things inside it." She pulled out some clothes that belonged to a woman and a few pictures. I moved closer to her and sat beside her on the floor.

"Lily, do you know your mother's first name?" She took out book after book, setting it on the floor between us.

"She had a name like mine," she said. She picked up a book and opened it, filled with pictures and old drawings. Some of the drawings were portraits of her ancestors.

"Like you? You mean Lilian or Lily?" I asked as she showed me a picture of her mother. She was beautiful with dark brown skin, but I couldn't tell if it was the picture or if her skin glowed.

"No, silly. Like my name. She said we all are flowers, but I called her mommy," she smiled. Lily handed me another photo of her as a baby. A man held her while a woman, her mother, smiled at them. The man was handsome but looked so familiar.

"Lily, what is your whole name?"

"Lilian Grace Cross- Vaughn," she smiled.

"Yes, that is a big name for a big girl, but I mean before your mommy and daddy gave you that name," I asked, reaching for another book. I opened it and found more drawings and some passages. As I looked through, something familiar started scratching at the back of my senses. I recognized these people. I flipped through and looked at the picture of the man holding baby Lily.

"Oh! Lilian Grace Butler." As Lily giggled, I looked at her with astonishment.

"Butler? You are from the Butler pack?" Her smile grew brighter. This could be the answer we need to stop the nonsense that is coming our way.

"Yes, Bibi. Of course, I am," I smiled just as brightly as she did at that news.

***

TARIA

I could feel it when Michael was close, and I knew he would do what he could protect the innocent. I was losing blood, but that is what also saved me. Maybe not from the claws and teeth of the panthers, but the damn Condemned who touched me. I couldn't wait any longer because the burn Masika's pain gave me hurt more than the claws and teeth. I had to do something to end this because we all would die if not. I refused to let that happen. I may be a vampire and have the power of the Impundulu, but I was always a Hunter first.

I whispered the healing tongue my father taught me. I was so happy to accept his training because even my blood or Impundulu wound this wound. I could feel it spreading across my shoulder and to my chest. It was trying to reach my heart, but I wasn't having that shit. My chanting grew stronger, and I could feel the lightning again in my veins, in my blood, calling me to use it. I asked my father where he learned this language, but he would say that we, the Cross family, are blessed with it. I don't know how I knew, but the translation of those words roughly came out as what I knew as a prayer.

"Give me such confidence in the power of your grace that even when I am afraid, I may put my complete trust in you."

I closed my eyes and pushed up. I could hear the lightning snap as everybody atop me disintegrated into dust. I stood up and could feel the blood leaking from every wound, but I knew they were closing up. The entire campus was filled with bright white light as I looked around. I moved, and it was faster than I thought I had ever gone. The panthers and Condemned, still alive, were caught in the light, almost as if they were paralyzed. I held my short sword out as I moved. I went from creature to creature and took them out where they stood. I could feel the light fade as everything snapped back into focus, and all the bodies that my blade touched fell to the ground, and I was the only one left standing.

The campus was quiet, but only because I didn't think everyone caught up with it being over.

I saw a few people who were down, but they seemed to be in some stasis type. I felt cool arms around my waist and Michael's power flow over me. I turned back to him and hugged him tight, but I knew we didn't have time for all that. I had to check on Jason and Leila. I had to make sure these people were going to be ok.

"How did you know?" I asked as I pulled away from him.

"Oh, I was coming any damn way, but you know how our family has a sixth sense about things," he said.

"Where are Jason and Leila? We need to get these people to a hospital." I said frantically. The winds were dying down, and the storm was receding. Now I could hear the cries and moans of the people. I knew I wouldn't be able to return to school if this was going to happen. Everything isn't the same anymore, and it doesn't matter how much I want it to be. I will always be a target, so I had to devise a better way. I won't let anyone dictate my life or harm the people I contact, including the so-called family.

"Help will be arriving soon, and I have called our people to get the ones who were most affected. As for your friends, they are over there." I looked where he pointed, expecting to see a headless body, but instead, I saw Leila holding her hands over Jason's broken and bleeding body. I started for Jason when I heard my name being called.

"Taria, Cross! Is this what you mean by being peaceful? Your kind has done nothing but bring death and pain to humans." My mouth almost fell open at Agent Hood's words. I felt Michael go still, and a low growl leaves his lips.

"Please get Jason out of here. I don't want them taking him." Michael looked down at me before he turned to do what I asked. I could handle Agent Hood and his bullshit. Instead of checking on my friends, I

took one step and was instantly in his face. I was hurt, covered in blood and wounds, because I was fighting to protect everyone, even his ass.

"Let me explain something to you, Agent Hood. I did everything possible to save who I could and keep everyone else out of danger. Those things that attacked us well and could do it again. The next time I may not be here to stop it. The world is changing, Mr. Hood, and it is getting more dangerous, but we are not the enemy," I growled.

I stepped back. I could feel the cameras on my back and hear the whispers through the crowd. "You may not want our help even after we save this world from being attacked and consumed, but you do not speak for everyone. I am not your enemy, but if you keep pushing Agent Hood, my services and the services of my people will no longer be given. Make your choice." I turned to see people watching our exchange and shook my head at the cameras that made it through all this. I looked at each person my eyes could reach and told them the truth.

"My people and I are not enemies. I was here because I discovered his organization had stolen one of our people. They claim they were helping him but lost him and blamed us for their wrongs. We are here to help, but I don't know if I can trust those who claim to be in charge. Everyone saw what we fought that night, and you saw us win. So, I say you need to choose whether you want our help. Yes, this is all new to some of you and maybe not to others, but what we will face will be like never before. I fought for you that night and fought for everyone here today, including Agent Hood. We have extended our help to the government, but Agent Hood's words are what we get. So, I am going to say this shit one more time. The world is changing and getting more dangerous, but we are not the enemy. Make your choice because that night will only be the beginning. Evil knows that everyone has seen its face close up now. It will kill, hurt, and sway some people to its side, but it will not stop. You want our help, or leave it to Agent Hood and his people to protect you. I will be listening."

I could feel Michael next to me as I spoke. My words were his words, and they were for everyone to hear. We stood together so everyone, including all supernaturals, that we were one. I turned to look up at him, and we both took one step and were gone before anyone could ask a question.

Chapter Twelve

TARIA

I followed Michael as we made our way through the streets, passing people by, when I felt my arm being pulled into an alley. "What the hell?" I said as Michael had me pressed against the wall.

"How did you stop that poison fire from reaching your heart?" Michael mumbled into my ear. I could feel how still his body was, but I could hear the shake in his voice. His spicy scent filled my nose, and my fangs pressed against my gums.

"It's a Hunter thing," I said, almost breathless. I was alive but lost a massive amount of blood, and I knew I had to feed before going home. Michael lifted his head and looked in the direction we came from.

"Amya and Winston, along with some of the turned vampires, have taken the people the panthers injured. It could become a panther, and we will give them a better chance to survive." I heard everything he was saying, but all I could think about was sinking my fangs into his neck. He turned back toward me, picked me up, and held me between the wall and his body.

"Drink, Taria." His blood pulsed in my ears, and I couldn't speak. He leaned his neck to the side, and my fangs slid down, and I drank. I knew he would stop me if I took too much, but I also knew my blood and fangs could hurt him as well. "Not anymore. You can take what you need from me now." I heard the words, but already I was sated. I didn't think that I took much, but his blood was different now, more powerful and rich. I pulled back, licking at his neck before I spoke. My mind was clearing, and his words from a few minutes ago flooded back.

"Where are they taking them?" I asked.

"To our brand-new hotel we own downtown," he said, stepping back and letting my feet hit the ground. I could still feel the burning, but it wasn't as bad, and I knew I would have to have my father look at it.

"A hotel? Why the hell do we have a damn hotel?"

"We need it for hosting our crowning, and because I refuse to keep anyone, I don't trust on our property."

"Ok. Ok, that is another conversation. What happened to Jason?" I asked, and he sucked his teeth and stepped back some more. His face screwed up before he looked back in my direction.

"I got Leila back to the truck while you spoke to Agent Hood, who is fucking up a treaty that has been in place long before he was born. Anyway, I had Leila take him back to the house and to your mother."

"The house? Why not the hotel?" I asked. I watched as his eyes flashed gold before dimming again before he spoke.

"He put himself in harm's way to buy you some more time, so I owe him. All debt is paid when his life is saved, and he makes it through his becoming," he growled. I wanted to smile but didn't want to push his goodwill.

"Well, I guess we should get back to the house then."

"Yeah, 'cause his ass is getting the hell out once he is on his feet. Helping you or not, he still has thoughts I am trying not to kill him over." I shook my head.

"Let's go, old man. Tell me, was there a Druid as well?" We walked toward my car as sirens filled the air.

"Yeah. I saw the Druid pull your aunt through the portal," Michael said as we stepped back onto the street. I looked up at him, knowing he thought the same damn thing I was.

"This bitch is working with fucking Apu."

"That is true, but there is something else I don't think you realize," he said as we hit the corner. I could see my car up ahead, and I thought back to the entire scene, trying to see what the hell I could have missed.

"What? I don't know what you mean?" My brows knitted together in thought.

"That's because you are still a new vampire. You are powerful, Taria, but you are still new to this life. You are not using all your gifts and senses that you have. Maybe that's too harsh. You do not know all your gifts and senses because we haven't had time to sit and learn. When I hit the scene on campus, I could smell not only Masika but Beverly as well. From what we know now about those two, I think those two are working together."

"Those no-good bitches," I growled. I stopped in place as the entire scene played through my mind. I analyzed each movement, scent, and a word spoken. Then I caught it, and it hit me like a ton of bricks. Not only did I smell Beverly, but I also caught a scent I wasn't expecting.

"What is it?"

"I think they have Luke, or they helped Luke escape." Michael went so still to where even I thought he was a statue.

"You're right. So that means either they are holding him captive or he is working with them, and by them, I mean Apu." I looked at

Michael, knowing he was right. We didn't need to look for him because he was already running with the enemy.

"Let's get back home. You need to change and check on your boy." I pulled out my keys and hit the button. We jumped in the car and peeled out. I knew from waking up that this day would be some bullshit, but I could already tell that the rest of the day would be just as bad. Something else would go down, and I want to be in the position to have the upper hand. I refuse to be caught off guard again. I heard Michael's phone buzz and saw him looking over his message.

"What is it now?" I asked as I switched lanes.

"Jason is definitely going to change, and Cam's parents just arrived." I jumped on the highway and shook my head. I looked at my clothes and cursed my aunt for messing up my first meeting with Caleb and Angelic Sloane.

"Why now?"

Joziah

I sat on the far edge of the property as I chanted in words no other human knew unless you were a Cross. My mind was open, and I could feel my thoughts reaching out to every Hunter in every family. I had no way of closing off the call to Beverly, but what she wouldn't do is to be able to pass through for the meeting. I laid layer after layer of protection around the realm where we would all meet. The only way to do it is if your blood is pure and you stand with the true Hunter ways. Each mind I touched was full of surprise and skepticism since I had been gone for so long. Many will show because of who I am, and others will show to make sure I am who I am.

I could feel every Hunter alive. They all knew what was at stake. Either you show up and declare your allegiance to the Hunter code or are with Beverly and what she wants. My call was sent, and the message was received. It would be to see who will be on the right side of this and who will be our enemy.

"Joziah!" I opened my eyes and got to my feet. I turned toward the house and could feel the panic coming from Naki in waves.

"Naki! What the hell is going on?" I started for the house but couldn't figure out what it could be. This land was now warded, and no one could cross onto it unless a select few permitted it.

"Joziah, hurry. I am going to need help with this one!" I rushed through the doors and entered the kitchen. The girl Leila, who looked to be of the Moon elf clan, helped Naki drag a young man onto the table.

"What the hell? Who is this?" I moved over to Naki as she ripped open the man's shirt while Leila held pressure on his neck. By the look of it, a were-panther attacked the man. I looked at Naki and saw the flash in her eyes.

"This is Jason, remember? The FBI Agent," she said, looking over his broken wrist and the puncture wound around his neck.

"What happened?" I asked the girl who looked to be Elven. She looked at me, but nothing came from her lips. "What happened? Where is Taria?" I asked again. I took out a blade when Naki held out her hand. I made a small neat slice in her skin, and she placed it over the wounds in his neck.

"Ahh. Some crazy-ass attacked .. were panther shifters. Taria is ok... Michael came, and shit just went crazy. He told me to get him here," she exclaimed.

"Joziah, this boy's injuries were done by–"

"Masika!" I turned, wanting to go for my daughter because if she was around, so was her damn mother.

"Joziah! You know our daughter is safe. She isn't alone, and she is strong. She would want us to help her friend." I didn't know how Naki could be so calm, but she knew our daughter better than I did. I was gone for far too long.

"I can help heal, but what can you do, Naki? He will be off her line. If and that is strong, if he makes it through the transformation, I don't know if we can trust him." We all looked back at Jason when he moaned. His entire body shook, and you could see his bones moving beneath his skin.

"I am not going to let this child die, Joziah." I looked at my pearl and saw her fangs grow as she partially shifted. She turned, moving so fast I didn't see when she sank her teeth into the boy's chest. I heard the crack as her teeth entered his heart. I knew this would probably be the only way he would survive and the only to save him from being a part of that line. Naki was strong and more powerful than her sister. And he will have a fighting chance. We just would have to wait and see.

"AHHHHH! AHHHHH!" Jason screamed, but Naki did not move. I helped Leila hold him down and to keep him as still as possible. I placed my hands around his broken wrist and whispered healing words, and Naki's blood helped heals the wounds on his throat. The thrashing calmed, and Naki pulled away.

"Joziah, his blood is slightly tainted. It has an essence of the demon and one we have dealt with before." I pulled my hand away from his wrist. I moved to let Naki take over, holding him down as I made a long thin cut on my hand. Jason's mouth was open, eyes wide, but he couldn't see. I knew all he felt at this moment was pain. I held my hand over his mouth, letting my blood drip down his throat to rid whatever taint was left inside him.

I moved my hand when his mouth slammed shut, and his entire body froze, half arched off the table. He slammed back down and went completely still.

"Do you need any help?" I turned to see a very tall man with a deep bass voice. His long dreads fell way past his waist. He looked enough like Camron and Marcus for me to figure out exactly who he was.

"Caleb Sloane, right?"

"Yes." He said, looking at me as if he should remember me.

"Good. Then yes, we need your help with healing. This boy will need all the help he can get." I turned back and prayed that Masika didn't have another panther joining her ranks because I didn't want to kill him.

KATHERINE

Lily talked as I went through each of the books she took out of her chest. We both snapped our heads up when the smell of blood hit the air, and the screaming started. I stood and grabbed Lily's hand when Garrett ran into the room. His eyes found Lily, and then he looked at me. "Garrett, I want you to stay with Lily until I return. I am going to go see what is going on." I patted Lily's hand, and Garrett came all the way into the room.

"Yes, ma'am. I think everything is ok but... I can't really see everything. You know?" He shrugged. I smiled as other scents filled my nose. I could tell not only was an unknown person in our home, but my brother was there as well, and I wasn't sure if I was ready to face him just yet.

"It's ok, Garrett, and we aren't meant to see everything." I moved to the door quickly. Stepping out, I saw a few wolves that stayed behind to help protect this place. "Please stay on this level and protect the children. Just in case." I said.

"No problem. We will ensure no one we don't know will make it up here." The young female wolf said.

"Thank you."

I turned, and all but levitated down the stairs, and when I entered the room, I saw my brother removing a lock of his hair. I watched as he squeezed the hair into a fine dust that glowed with a pearly luminescence. He placed his hand over the boy's chest, where large bite wounds were. The boy went still once more, and everyone turned my way.

"Brother," I said. Before I knew it, he held me in his arms.

"I thought you were dead." My eyes were closed, but I could hear everyone gathering the man at the table. I had no idea where they were taking him, but I hoped he wasn't staying in this house. Not with my grandchildren here within these walls. I hugged him tightly, taking in his familiar scent and strength. I pulled myself back together and pushed away from him to look into his eyes.

"I am very much alive." I frowned and stepped back. I folded my arms over my stomach because, for the life of me, I didn't know why my brother let this happen.

"Kat? What is wrong? You look at me as if I were a stranger." The hurt across his face hit my slowly beating heart, but it couldn't matter. I heard light footsteps behind me, and I turned to face Angelic.

"Katherine? Gods, it is true!" The happiness in her eyes died the moment I stepped away. "What the hell is going on here?" She asked, looking between my brother and me. "Katherine, we thought you were dead. Everyone thought you were dead." I swallowed. The entire time I was in that room wasn't spent in self-pity. Most of it was the thought that my own family let what happened to my children go down. Caleb stepped forward with a frown, and I looked up into his eyes.

"Talk to me, twin." Tears burned the backs of my eyes, but I held them at bay. I took in a breath and closed my eyes. When I opened them, I was calm.

"How in the hell could you let the Van Allan family take my child? Your nephew! How did you not know I was alive? My problem is you never looked for me. You let those people take my children and use them!"

"They were the next ruling family until Michael became—"

"You are his family! You knew we didn't trust them, and I told you something wasn't right. You didn't want to listen," I growled. I could feel my blood boil and heat.

"Katherine, this is not our fault! You will not speak to my kindred in this—" Angelic started.

"Kindred!" I laughed. The bitterness in my mouth had me shaking my head.

"Yes, my Kindred Soul! Your brother—"

"Let me ask you this, brother, did you accept things as they were because your beloved wife is a Van Allan herself?" It felt as if the world went quiet. I was glad it did because, yes, I was back, and the lies from the past would be revealed. Angelic always wanted to rule, and she schemed more than her damn brothers, but mine never could fucking see it. I know for a fact that whoever is trying to take out Taria is a part of it in some way. I won't let her stop Taria and Michael's reign.

Chapter Thirteen

JOZIAH

I knew while he transformed that Taria and Michael wouldn't want him inside the house. For whatever reason, Michael gave him the ok to be here, and I guessed because he knew the only chance he had was Naki.

"I hope this works," Naki said. We made it to where we kept Quan when he was a danger. I held onto Jason with the help of Leila while Naki opened one of the cell doors. She made the bed as comfortable as possible, but it wouldn't matter.

"Naki, let it be." She moved out of the way, and Leila and I placed him inside.

"I will stay until he wakes." I looked down at Leila and back to Naki. "Don't worry. I will stay outside of the cell doors. I could handle myself if he were to get loose." She looked back down at Jason and stood.

"Ok. Thank you, Leila. I want to say I had no idea you—" Naki said when Leila laughed.

"It's ok, Mrs. Pearl. I believe it was all meant to be this way." We closed the doors, and I laid extra protection around the lock.

"Naki, I need to finish what I was doing, but I think you should check on Katherine. I feel she isn't happy about her brother. His wife is here." I turned to leave when I felt a small hand on my arm.

"Mr. Cross? I... I told Taria about my family and what–" She never finished her statement because Jason began screaming again. I reached out to stop her, but she entered the cell.

"Leila!" I screamed, but Naki grabbed her.

"Wait! I can help him through the pain! Just let me go. Please!" She cried. Naki looked at me, but what could I say? I could see the bond that was connecting them, but I don't think she even noticed yet.

"Naki, let her be. Leila, if it becomes dangerous to get out of the cell and comes and gets us at once." I commanded. She stared into my eyes and saw I wasn't giving her a choice. I would remove her if needed.

"Yes, sir," she said as Naki let her go. She went to Jason, and Naki closed the cell door again and came to me.

"Are you sure about this, Joziah?"

"Could anyone have kept you from me?" I asked. She turned to look into my eyes.

"No." I kissed her as Taria and Michael stepped onto the property.

Taria

As soon as we entered the gate, I could feel the tension on our land. I just wanted to see my kids, shower, and eat food. Maybe a large steak and some potatoes with a glass of wine. In fact, a large glass of wine is in order after this damn day.

"Are you listening to the conversation that's going on in the house, or do you think about food?" Michael asked.

"Whatever, asshole. I had a very long day, and I'm hungry! Why, what the hell is going on that can't wait until I take a shower?"

"You must get over not listening to other people's conversations. It will always help with self-preservation."

"You forget I didn't grow up with these gifts. It will take me a minute to conform to your vampy ways."

"Are you serious? Vampy ways?"

"What!" I asked as we pulled outside the doors. I knew his ass was trying to keep me from not listening to what was happening, but it was too late. I watched as the front doors opened, and my baby girl came running down the steps with tears in her eyes. "Aww hell naw!" I closed the car door, stepped away, and fell to one knee. I opened my arms, and Lily ran into them.

"Mommy... mommy, she—" Lily cried. I looked up at Michael, who stood in front of Garrett. The two weren't saying a word to each other. I knew my son was going to be creepy like his damn father.

"Lily, calm down. Everything is ok. I'm ok. Your daddy is ok. Why are you so upset?" Michael snapped his head and looked toward me and back to the house. Before I could open my mouth, he was gone, and the front door was closing again.

"What the hell?" I said, standing up with Lily in my arms. Once he said something about listening in the car, I started to. I didn't hear anything before, but Katherine was demanding answers. I didn't hear the answers that were given. "Lily, baby, let me take you to your room and find out what's happening."

"No! Bibi doesn't like that lady, mommy. She feels wrong." I looked at Garrett.

"What do you have to say about this?" He knew something by the look of sadness on his face.

"I think you should let dad handle this."

"I think you should answer my question." I snapped with raised brows. He looked down but shook his head.

"Yes, ma'am." While holding Lily, I walked over to him and ran my fingers through his hair.

"Talk to me, Garrett," I whispered as the voices got quieter inside the house.

"I'm not sure, but I don't think that lady likes you, and I think she had something to do with dad's brother being killed. The dream is all so confusing now." His voice was a whisper, but I heard every word.

"It's ok, baby. We will figure all this out. Don't worry about a thing. I don't think she could have anything to do with that, but don't worry so much." Lily sniffed and lifted her head to look at me.

"She doesn't like Bibi," Lily whispered. It took me a minute to figure out who she was talking about. I realized she was talking about Katherine, but it made little sense. Caleb and Angelic are more than just Blue Bloods; they are family.

I took Lily and Garrett back to their rooms, and the wolves nodded as we passed.

"Taria, Katherine asked us to watch them, but when you pulled up, we thought it would be ok to let them go to you," Shani said, looking over the two.

"It's cool, Shani, and you did the right thing. Please do me a favor and keep them busy while we sort this out. I will ask my mother or father to make something to eat for everyone."

"Sure, that's no problem. Your parent went to help that elf chick with the new shifter."

"Thanks. I will shower quickly and try to figure out what's happening. Have you heard from Toya or Quinn?" I asked.

"The Alpha said we would follow Alpha Dax's command until return. Toya contacted me through a mirror." She said, shaking her head. "She said she tried you, but you must have been busy. She wants you to call her."

"Ok, so she on some real witchy shit. Thanks, Shani." I smiled and turned to go up the stairs to our room.

I showered and dressed in a pair of my standard black leggings, knee boots, and a long-sleeved V-neck, deep purple sweater. Toya gave this to me before she left and told me it had good karma or some shit. I ran a waffle brush through my hair and pulled it back into a bun. I wanted to make a good impression on Camron's parents so he wouldn't give me shit when he came home. I knew they would have to be in the meeting room because not even Michael could hear through those walls. He probably would just listen in on thoughts anyway because he gives no damn personal space. I reached for the door, my stomach rang, and mild nausea overcame me.

"I must starve and more nervous than I thought," I muttered. I wanted to learn about Jason and talk to my father and mother about who showed up today, but I knew this was slightly more important. Why would Lily and Garrett say things like that about people they have never met? In any case, I would take their feelings over people I didn't know any damn day. The door swung open, and Michael stared down at me.

"I want you to meet my uncle and aunt." His face gave away nothing, and he didn't even try to talk to me telepathically. I didn't try either because his eyes and body told me all I needed. Someone in this room is very strong in that skill and will probably read my thoughts if they feel us communicating. His eyes squinted, and I could see their anger and confusion. They weren't burning gold, but that honey brown and sexy ass lips sat in a straight line.

"Ok. I got you. Let's do this," I said with a smile. He stepped back, letting me walk in, and instantly I felt exactly what the hell my children were talking about. Sorry, Cam and Marcus, but I don't think I will like this bitch.

"Well, it is finely nice to meet you, Hunter." Angelic smiled.

MASIKA

After the Druid took me to its Master, he dropped me back at the house where Beverly, and I held up. My chest burned with every movement, but the deal was made, and it was a good one. My heart is for power. Once I get my mother's heart, I will get my heart back. I didn't know why Apu wanted my heart instead of my soul, but it didn't matter. I would have it back with my love once everything is said and done.

"What the hell happened to you?" Beverly sneered in my direction. Her Hunters stood at attention throughout the house, as did my panthers.

"Things didn't go to plan, but no matter. I have a better one." I hissed as the burning in my veins intensified.

"You look like shit, but that has nothing to do with me. Everything is going according to my plan, so make sure you hold up the end of your deal. I don't have time to babysit a child who is still heartbroken over a long-dead—" I struck out with my claws, but she moved just in time. I looked down at my hand and saw the long black claws. The tips curved at the end of each nail.

"That's new," I whispered to myself. I saw the Hunters next to Beverly holding their weapons' hilts. My panthers looked at me confused but were ready and waiting for my command. "Don't fucking worry about me, Beverly. I can handle my own shit. Just worry about how you will get someone who doesn't give two shits about you to love you." I spat. I pulled myself together and turned around.

"Make sure, Masika, you don't extend yourself too far. Making too many deals will always bite you in the ass." I didn't reply. I knew what I needed to do and how to do it. Taria and Michael are more powerful than I thought, but I almost had her when she was alone. I just had to figure out how to keep them apart.

Michael

"Well, it is finely nice to meet you, Hunter," Angelic smiled. I was about to let my aunt know who she was talking to, but Taria was ahead of the game. I felt her hand brush mine as she moved passed me.

"Yes. I agree that it is finally nice that you have met me. Camron and Marcus haven't said anything about you, but I am glad we can finally get to know one another," Taria said with a smile. She stood directly in front of Angelic without extending her hand. She looked over and up to Caleb, and a large smile spread across her lips. "You must be Caleb. Cam has told me so much about you. I am so happy to meet you." I watched as she reached out, and Caleb was surprised but hugged her back with a smile.

"He was probably making up lies about me. It is good to meet you, Queen Taria." He chuckled. I looked over at my mother, and a small smile played on her lips.

"Oh, please call me Taria or Hunter. That works as well since I am that as well." She sent a side-eyed to Angelic before stepping back. "Now, all that is out of the way. Let's talk about what the hell was going on when we pulled up. Cause I will tell you right now, I don't like chaos in my home, and I do not like coming home to a crying child." She was smiling, but that shit was frosty. Whatever Lily and Garrett said to her already had her backup. I moved forward because it didn't look like my mother would say anything to stop.

"Taria, these three were just about to fill me in on the problem, right?" I said, letting the command lace through my words. I stood behind Taria, and I felt her step back and press her body against mine. It helped to calm me down and probably her as well.

"I can tell you now, Michael, she is going to be a problem," Angelic said, rolling her eyes.

"I can't find a problem with my Kindred Soul being my Queen aunt Angelic," I said, trying but failing hard as fuck from not growling.

"Michael, I know what she is to you, but she is a Hunter. No vampire is going to agree to follow–"

"Angelic! That conversation is Blue Blood council business. This is family business, and I want to know why my sister is saying the things that she is." The bass in his voice boomed across the room. I couldn't agree more with him, but the fact she went right in on the whole Hunter shit had me thinking twice about a woman I knew my entire life.

"I agree with my uncle." I turned to my mother, and she moved forward, looking every bit at the Queen she was, and narrowed her eyes.

"I want to know why my brother never looked for his King or me. I want to know why my sons were left in the hands of Peter and Victor Van Allan. Like my twin brother, I want to know why you could not feel I was still alive. None of this is making any sense to me, and I want it cleared up and right damn now." The growl in her voice had Taria reaching out for her hand. Her fangs were long, and her skin glowed with power. As she spoke, I kicked myself for never having the exact same thoughts. I turned back, wanting the answers because something wasn't fucking right.

Chapter Fourteen

TARIA

I could tell shit was getting real. I held Katherine's hand tightly, and I could feel her shaking. I didn't think it was in fear but in anger. Her words made me look at all this shit in a different light. Things have been hitting us non-stop and back to back. We never had a moment to sit down and think. We never had a moment to analyze what happened all those years ago. I never asked Michael what happened that night and why he left with the Van Allan family. I looked over my shoulder, and I could see he was thinking along my lines.

There was something wrong with this picture, and it was time to figure this shit out now. We have enemies all around us, and we don't need more of them. I watched Angelic as she blinked fast and held out her hands.

"Ok, let's back this up a moment. We are family here and have known each other for quite a long time." She looked at me with a dismissive gaze. Katherine squeezed my hand when I almost slapped the hell out of her. "Well, most of us. Let's all sit down and talk about this—" We all turned at the loud knocking on the door. The person on the other side didn't wait but just pushed it open. I wasn't worried because I knew it was my father.

"I know this is a bad time, Taria, but we need to talk," Joziah said. He lifted her head, nodded to Caleb, and flicked his eyes over Angelic.

"Can you give me a few minutes or—"

"No. This is important, and we need to deal with this as soon as possible." My father said, holding my eyes. I turned back around to look at Michael when his phone rang and my own. "Shit."

"We can finish this up later. Taria handles your business. I am going to see what this is all about." Michael said as he answered his phone. I pulled mine out of my pocket and answered while following my father out of the meeting room.

"Yes. Hello, who is this?" I said. My father was moving quickly through the house, heading to his and my mother's rooms.

"Taria, what the hell is going on?"

"Toya?" I looked back at the phone, not recognizing the number she was calling from.

"Who else would it be?" She snorted.

"Ahh... any damn body because I don't know this number!" I said. I watched as my father waved a hand over his door and entered. I followed close behind and saw my mother pulling some items out of old trunks.

"Ahh shit, I am getting good. I saw how I could use my powers to affect technology, but that isn't the reason I'm calling."

"What's up? There is a lot of—"

"Cause you are all over the damn news yet again! What the hell is going on? Do I need to come back?"

"LaToya, Taria, and Michael can handle their own shit. Stop trying to jump in the middle of things. Not long ago, you were running scared of your shadow," Quinn said in the background.

"Shut the hell up, Quinn. I just didn't do that whole paranormal stuff. I didn't think that shit was real. Give me a break." Toya said. I could hear her hitting Quinn, but we both knew that shit didn't hurt him. He just laughed.

"Toya, I'm good. It's a lot of things happening right now, but I'm good."

"People are talking, girl. Some are good, and others are not so hot. I just heard a poll say you have a seventy-six percent approval rating nationwide. But global percentage, girl, you sittin' at ninety-two percent approval. I know you may not want to hear this, but you may need to do another sit-down interview. I will agree that you were right about the first one." I took in a breath because I realized I wasn't breathing. I looked up to see my mother and father watching me with interest.

"That is something I will think about, and I am glad you admitted that I was right and you were wrong."

"Ha, ha, ha, but be serious, Taria. Are you ok because I will make a portal and coming to you if you need me? I know you can handle yourself because you did that before getting my powers, but we are still besties, and I am your Witch. You know what to do if the time comes and you need us."

"I do. Don't worry, bitch. I got this. If shit gets crazy, I will hit you up."

"Aight. I hear you talking. We are almost to the first pack we see, so I will call soon."

"Ok. Be safe and kiss my babies." I discounted the call and looked up. "What's going on?"

"The call has been answered, and Hunters are arriving. We need to go."

"Ok. Where exactly are we going?"

"The Other lands. Listen, Taria. Everything will be fine. This isn't the first time humanity has discovered how thin the veil is with supernatural kind. It will all work out, baby girl. The last time it happened, Hunters were made, and now this time, you are here. There is always a reason. We have to deal with what is in front of us now. That is Beverly, Masika, and Apu." I couldn't look away from their eyes. They were so much like my own as he spoke. I knew he was right and had to get my head into the game.

"I got you, dad. Are we ready to go? Mom, what do you have?" I asked, looking behind my father. I looked on the bed at the weapons and clothing she laid out for my father. I walked over and picked up a black long-sleeved shirt. It was old, and I couldn't tell what type of material it was made from. I turned it around, and the same symbol was also on the back.

"What is this?" I asked. I felt as if I was drawn to it. The longer I stared at it. I could see the fire moved.

"That is over the family's crest. That is your crest." I held up the shirt and looked over the blue moon thereat was surrounded by fire. It seemed to get brighter and brighter the longer I stared at the fire.

"It's alive," I whispered.

"That it is. Our Hunter line was born doing a Full Blue Moon, and it was said that when we were given gifts, heaven's fires encircled that moon. That is how it has become our family crest." My father said as he walked ours to me. I couldn't take my eyes off the moon, and it was as if I could see the day it happened. I felt warm hands cover my own as my father pushed mine down.

"Sorry... I just–"

"No need. You can have it. I have another, and I will make you more."

"I can't fit this thing. I have some weight, but this thing is huge," I laughed.

"It will be a perfect fit. Trust me." He leaned over and kissed my forehead, just like he used to do when I was younger. "Look closely at your blades and swords you got from our basement. You will find that same crest on each one somewhere. Now get dressed and meet me at the far edge of the back of the property in ten minutes." He moved away, picked up some clothes, and entered the bathroom. I looked at my mother, but she stared unseeing out of the window.

"We will get her mom. I promise," she turned with a smile.

"I know, baby. I want you to be careful. This feud was long before you were born, so don't think it's all about you. All of you did what was necessary to save innocent people. I just want to find my brother."

"You haven't felt anything else?" I asked.

"No, not yet. Don't worry, Taria. I will deal with that. Go and get ready and love on your children before you go." I didn't want to leave because of the sadness in her eyes. I knew when not to push her, either. I turned and headed for the door.

"Oh! How is Jason? Did he–"

"We will see. Everything is fine right now. Go and handle what you need to."

"Ok. Please tell me what happens, no matter what," I said with a smile.

"I will. I promised I wouldn't keep things from you again, and I meant that." I moved back and gave her a kiss on the cheek. I left the room and started preparing myself for the gathering of Hunters.

Michael

I watched as Taria exited out of the room, and I answered the call. I wouldn't have picked up if it wasn't Camila calling me because I wanted to know exactly what was happening.

"Yes," I answered. I watched as Angelic went over to speak with my mother.

"Michael, the covens are arriving. You and Taria need to get down here as soon as possible. There have already been grumblings about our Queen, but I hear more and more about the kids." I looked over at my mother, conversing quietly with my aunt. Maybe being away has messed with her mind because I know for sure that one of her answers is easy. There is no way her brother could be against us. That would be too much for her, Camron, Marcus, and me.

"I will be right there."

"And, Taria?" Her voice went up an octave. I could hear the frustration in her tone, but Taria had to handle her Hunter business.

"She will meet me later. My mother will accompany me. Ensure the ballroom is ready and everything is as it should be."

"I can't believe this!"

"Believe it!" I growled. The line went quiet for a minute, but I knew she was still there.

"There is one other problem," she said in a more controlled tone. I closed my eyes, trying to see what else could be happening.

"Just tell me, Milly." I used her old nickname she hated as a child.

"I haven't heard that in over–"

"It has been a while, I know. Just tell me because it isn't meant for me to see," I said as quietly as possible.

"There has been a request that some top officials from the government would like to be here. After you and Taria pulled that stunt on camera today, they want to know if what she said is true. How can we come to an agreement?"

"Sara's trial is tonight, Camila."

"This may be a perfect time. They held her son, and now he is still lost. That puts you and Taria in a better light because you did not execute a youngling, Blue Blood." I thought over her words, and I was glad about deciding to bring my mother. My father and mother have done this many times before.

"Fine. I want them in another part of the hotel away from the covens. I also want every piece of information on who will attend. I will not be blind." I ended the call and turned to see Angelic and my uncle leaving the room.

"So, I guess it is time for me to get back out there if I heard you correctly," my mother asked.

"Yes. I would really love your expertise in dealing with these idiots," she smiled, and a flash of fang shone in the light.

"We need to dress for the occasion. Rule number one in dealing with the idiots, as you call them, is always to look the part. You are the King, so you and your Queen will dress accordingly. I am sure Taria has gowns. I will lay one out for when she returns." At that, she turned on her heel and started for the door.

"Hold up. What is going on with that whole situation?" I asked. She stopped at the door and turned to look me in the eye.

"There are secrets you do not know, my son. There are Deadly Secrets about this world and family I thought were long dead. There is something I can't put my finger on, but it will hold until we deal with this tonight." At that, she turned and walked out of the door. I wish I knew how many more damn secrets would be revealed.

Angelic

I couldn't wrap my mind around that they actually let these wolves live in their homes. Two of them showed us to our rooms on the far-right wing of the house. It was grand, but filling it with all types of supernaturals was beneath a Pure or Blue Blood vampire.

"Thank you." I heard Caleb say to the wolves.

"It isn't any problem. Please let us know if you need anything." The young female wolf said. I heard the click of the door and turned around.

"What the hell is this madness?" I asked.

"I don't know. I want to know what my sister is thinking. I thought she was dead. I couldn't feel her." He said, pacing the room.

"No! No, not that. I mean the way that little Hunter bitch Taria spoke to me. You didn't even say anything!" I was livid, but I had to pull myself back. I had to stay calm.

"Well, you were very hostile, Angel. We really need to talk about what has been going on with you. You have been acting so strange lately. Also, watch your tongue and how you speak about our Queen. Just do as your sons ask and get to know her. She seems lovely to me as well." Caleb was a fool if he thought I would ever bow down to a Hunter.

"My sons know nothing." I stormed into the large connecting master suite and closed the doors. Turning, I saw a lovely decorated bathroom fit for royalty, and that is exactly what I was. He spoke of my sons, but Camron isn't telling me anything that is going on in his life. I have been hearing that he found his Kindred Soul, and that she is a shifter. If that is true, I would have to take things into my own hands because not one of my boys will lower themselves to sleep with dogs. I moved toward the huge mirror that covered most of the wall over the sinks. Looking into the mirror, I was happy at what I saw. I looked over my flawless honey-brown skin, beautiful gray eyes, slim body, and sharp ass fangs. I stared into those eyes and saw Angelic screaming in pain. I smiled as I waved my hand in front of the mirror and watched as it shimmered.

It was time to take things into my own hands because it seemed as if my so-called stepbrothers and stepfather were too stupid to accomplish anything. I blew at the mirror and whispered words that few spoke this day, and the glass liquified. I tapped the moving surface, which became still and showed me a face I hadn't seen in over a thousand years.

"Masika, circumstances bear changed, and I think I can help you," I said in greeting to the daughter of the head Witch in whose coven I belonged.

"Jinx is still running around in that body, I see. It is good to hear that you can help. So as you know, this has nothing to do with my mother. She knows nothing about what exactly I am doing." She said. Masika looked slightly different. Her eyes held a red tint, and her skin seemed ashen.

"When have we always told your mother everything we have done together? You helped me get who I deserved, and I helped you have a child by the one you loved."

"Yes, and that child is now dead!" She hissed.

"Yes, that is true, but we can get back at the ones who have wronged us. A child for a child sounds about right." I watched as a slow smile began to spread across her face, and I knew I had an ally in my fight.

Chapter Fifteen

TARIA

I figured I should dress comfortably, so I put on a pair of fitted black cargo pants and my all-black Nike boots. I reached out for the shirt and put it on over my head, knowing full well this damn thing was way too big. It didn't matter because it was something my father owned, and apparently, he made it. I stood up, pulling the large shift down, and felt a tingling sensation along my skin. I could feel my father all around me and what made up his powers. The fabric moved and stretched, forming my body's shape until it fits perfectly. The shining of the moon and fire faded until they were just outlined on the shirt. I moved around, but it felt like a part of me. "Damn," I whispered when I heard a soft knock at the door. I knew who it was because I heard their little voices coming down the hall. I walked to the door and pulled it open, revealing two faces I loved more each day.

"Mommy, where are you going?" Lily asked.

"Come help me pick out some weapons for my trip," I said.

"Are there going to be bad guys on this trip?" Lily asked, almost excited.

"Lily stop asking so many questions," Garrett said, taking my hand. I looked down but didn't say a word about it.

"It's cool, G. I don't mind," I said as we walked. My room with my favorite weapons wasn't fair, and Lily ran to open the door.

"I know, but I can't see if it will be trouble. It's making me mad, and I don't know how dad deals with this." He shook his head as we entered the room.

"Well, for starters, he is old, and with age comes patience," I said with a smile. Garrett and Lily fell into laughter, which was exactly what I wanted. I looked around to see which swords I wanted to take with me. I looked at my Katana but didn't feel right to bring her with me on this one. I looked over at the curved swords I loved so damn much, but they were right for this, either.

"You should take the twins," Garrett said, pointing to where Lily was standing.

"Yeah, mommy, I think these will look pretty when the moonlight hits them." I looked at the two and approached the twin Samurai dual blades.

"Ok, if you two say so, that's what it will be." I picked them up to feel them out, but I didn't need to. The weight was perfect. I turned it over to look at the hilt, and I saw the crest of my house and knew these were the right blades to take.

"Well, babies, I have to go, but I will be back. Listen to grandma and Shani. We will probably have to get ready to join your father at our brand-new hotel when I get home." I smiled, and Garrett rolled his eyes. Lily didn't smile for once, and her gaze took on a knowing one. At times her eyes looked so ancient for a young girl.

"We probably won't go right away, so I won't wear my new dress until later." She moved fast and wrapped her arms around my legs. I looked at Garrett, but he held a frown as well. I heard footsteps, and we all turned.

"Taria, let's move. Garrett, you're the man of the house. Take care of your sister and grandmother." My father said. Lily disengaged herself from me and ran to her poppa. I looked at Garrett, and he reached over and hugged me.

"I will make sure she stays out of trouble."

"Thanks. I love you." I kissed his head and started for my father. "Ok, let's do this," I said, and we kissed Lily on the cheek. I followed him in the setting sun to the back of our property. It was at the very far edges, and I didn't think my father could keep up with my speed, but I was so damn wrong.

"Not bad, Taria," he said, not winded at all.

"Damn, dad, aren't you like five thousand years old? You shouldn't have this much stamina," I laughed. He chuckled but didn't smile.

"Five thousand, you think?" He looked at me while holding his hands up to the sky. I raised a brow, trying to figure out exactly how old my parents were.

"Yeah..." I felt a sudden burst of energy and watched as my father moved his hands. He mumbled words that I shouldn't have been able to understand, but I did. The world felt like it shifted, and things got blurry, but it stopped before I could reach out to my father.

"Damn, that felt crazy," I said, looking myself over. I looked up at my father, who was staring into the sky. I followed his gaze and gasped at the dark sky that was only lit by a full blue moon with a fire burning around it.

"Add on a few more thousand, then come talk to me. Let's move." I turned to see him dash off into the woods, which had me blinking in shock for a moment. The moon shined like the sun, and I watched as the trees uprooted and parted.

"Ok, this is some Lord of the Rings type shit right here." I shook my head and followed the man I thought I would never see again.

It wasn't a long run, but it felt exhilarating. Every breath I took felt like I was breathing raw energy. "What is this place?" I asked when we both stopped at a large rock formation.

"This is a pocket of the Other lands. I formed this place and created a barrier for only the Hunters that are worthy shall pass between these two stones. I looked at the unusual stones that burned a sea-green color. As we approached, they glowed brighter.

"This is way beyond anything I have ever seen," I laughed, looking around.

"These rocks are Earth elementals. They live in this world and have agreed to let us gather here." When he said the words, I felt my necklace heat against my skin, making me reach for it. I pulled it out to look at the burning orange stone that Katara had given me.

"I guess they are communicating?" I asked.

"Yes. In a way, we don't have time to discuss that. Lessons on elemental another day, and then you will understand how rare of a gift you received.

"Ok. After you," I said with a smile. My father shook his head and turned. Before he moved us, both turned at a noise coming from the trees.

"Joziah!" I didn't know her well, but I knew exactly who she was when she emerged from the trees.

"Beverly." My father growled and moved before I could say a word.

JOZIAH

"What are you doing here?" I roared into her face. When I formed this pocket, I placed rules that everyone, including myself, had to follow.

"I heard the call just as everyone else, Joziah. I just wanted to see if we can settle this without a war?" Her fake smile hurt because we were once a student and teachers. Hell, we were friends, but she betrayed me and the entire world for fucking power.

"Everything you have done has pushed us to war, Beverly. You want to rule over the Hunters, but you don't even know the meaning of what we are here to do. My father made a mistake in naming your family name as one of us." The hate burned in my veins as the knowledge of what she had done played through my mind.

"We could run this supernatural world Joziah. They fear us, and they should. We are the checks and balance to their lives, so why shouldn't we run it?" I looked into her eyes. Her beauty was still there, but her soul was evil and rotten.

"You never understood our role on this Earth, Beverly. There is nothing more for us to talk about." I turned and left when I left Taria to come up beside me. I looked down and saw the raw fury on her face and her clenched fists.

"Well, hello, little Naki. Nice to see you all grown up," Beverly gritted.

"Stay the fuck away from my family. I know your role and what you were willing to have your children do. There will be war, Ryder. You best believe that," Taria growled in Beverly's face. I reached out, grabbing onto my daughter's hand. I pulled her back and wondered how she could get so close to her. She was a breath away, and I could tell Beverly also noticed. Beverly took a step back and smiled.

"Well, she does have a nice set of fangs on her. I guess like father like daughter. I don't know how you could lie with a creature—"

"I know this bitch, not—" I caught Taria by the waist, holding her tight to my chest. I didn't want to break my agreement with the Earth elementals.

"Calm yourself, baby girl," I whispered in her ear. She breathed hard, and I could feel each breath on my chest. I looked up, but Beverly was gone.

"If you or mom doesn't kill her soon, I'm taking that bitch out."

"Watch your mouth. I have no idea how you could try to attack her, but I need you to know that shouldn't be."

"What? Why?"

"I did not design it to be that way, but from here on out, control yourself. I do not want to break my agreement with these elementals. Whatever happens in this meeting, keep your cool, say whatever you want to, but keep your shit tight." I let her go and searched the woods once more.

"I got you," she whispered and shook herself. She jumped in place and cracked her neck before looking back at me.

"Ok. Let's go." We turned, and this time nothing stopped us from entering between the stones.

Chapter Sixteen

MICHAEL

I bite down on my irritation about being unable to drive to the hotel. I shifted into the black-on-black tux that I refused to wear the bow tie for.

"Get used to all this, Michael. You grew up doing this. It shouldn't be this hard," Katherine said with a half-smile.

"That was long ago, and I have moved on with the times. I didn't do the whole royal thing. That was Martin and Victor's thing," I said, fixing the cuff links Lily insisted I wear. The initials engraved on the platinum links were **GL**.

"Yes. That is not where I would have wanted you to be. Not with them," I nodded, but we didn't say more. One of the turned vampires was driving my white Rose Royce Ghost, and I didn't want to give him an ear of information.

"That is something we need to talk about." As we pulled up to the hotel, I felt the satisfaction of seeing my children's names stamped big as hell for all to see. Malia and Camila were standing at the doors when we pulled to a stop. Before the driver could move, I opened the door and reached out a hand to my mother. If humans were looking, they would never know who she was to me.

"Thank you." She said as Malia walked beside her into the building.

"This looks good, Camila. You outdid yourself."

"Yes, I did with your money, so it was easy. You know I like expensive things," she smiled as the camera flashed.

"Why are you allowing this?"

"Government officials are here, Michael. It is good for the city and world to see we weren't hiding. I got this. Just do your thing." She purred and turned away to speak with the press. My skin felt itchy when Taria crossed over for that meeting, and I wouldn't say I liked it. It reminded me of when she almost died, and that connection was lost. I went through the massive doors and saw my mother talking to a few Blue Bloods who couldn't believe she was still alive. I moved swiftly, trying not to be noticed, but that was asking for too much.

"Michael Vaughn King of Vampires. How I am glad we are finally here to crown you." I turned to see John Noble coming toward me with a smile.

"I am glad you could be here for it. Last I heard, you didn't like leaving England," I said as he bowed.

"Ahh, yes. I haven't liked these past few years, but things are getting more interesting. Where is our lovely new Queen?" He said, looking around.

"She will be here later," I said. "How about we get a drink, and you can tell me how your coven is handling our new situation," I said to change the subject.

"Yes, yes. That is something. I remember when all this happened last time, but I can tell you what I know." He winked. He was turned by Gio a little later in his years. You could tell by the head full of gray hair that he looked to be in his sixties at the time. As we moved away, I saw my uncle arrive through the doors. What had me stopping was the fact that Angelic wasn't with him.

"John, excuse me for a moment. I want to hear what you say, but I must greet my uncle."

"Yes, yes, not a problem." I took a step and ended up in front of my uncle. Most vampires didn't pay the show of speed any mind, but I could hear the gasps from the human attending to this thing.

"Caleb, where is Angelic? Why isn't she with you?" I asked. I had an itch in the back of my mind, but nothing was there when I looked for it. I tried to see the problem but was too close to the situation, which kept me on guard.

Taria

After I walked through the stones, my mouth fell open at the number of Hunters gathered. I had no idea it was this many, but it had to be if we were supposed to keep supernaturals from running wild worldwide. I felt my father before I saw him step up beside me.

"These are our people Taria. They have been misguided and lost. We must unite them and put them on the correct path as Hunters." We stood at the back of a crowd of Hunters, listening before we made a move for the raised stones at the front.

"I understand, dad. I don't want them to be afraid of me, but they will also understand that I am a vampire." I looked over all the Hunters in different colors and crests that marked their weapons and clothing. I ran my eyes over everyone and stopped when I saw the moon and fire. I look up to see a man who closely resembles my father. When he caught my eye, he was talking to a woman that wasn't much shorter than him. He stopped talking and looked me over before his light brown eyes shifted to my father.

"Joziah." The man said in a rush of air. All talking stopped, and Hunters turned around to face us.

"Yes, Joshua. It is me." My father said with a nod. I looked back and forth between the two and wondered if I had an uncle, I knew nothing about. Joshua moved, and the next thing I knew, he hugged my father tight before pushing him back to look him over again.

"I thought... I thought you were dead! What the hell... what?" I could see the questions in his eyes, but they were all coming out too fast for his mouth to speak.

"That is why I have called this meeting. I will tell you everything." My father said, clapping Joshua on the back. "I will tell all of you everything because we don't have time to fuck around." My father said as his smile faded. Joshua looked at me and back to my father, but we started walking so the meeting could start.

"That is her." I heard whispers coming from the crowd.

"I can't tell if she is or isn't a vampire. Her energy is all off." Another person said.

"Has anyone been watching the news? Of course, it's her. She is one of them. I saw her with him." Another person said. I turned toward the last comment making eye contact with that Hunter. I nodded but kept it moving as we made it to the front. My father jumped up and landed on the top stone. I followed along with Joshua and the woman next to him. She watched me cursorily but with no hate or judgment. My father stepped forward, but I quickly reached out to stop him. I knew people wanted to hear from him and know what the hell happened and where he was, but that isn't the main reason we were here. He looked down at me and gave a quick sharp nod. I saw the pride and approval flash in his eyes before I stepped forward.

"I know that some of you may have heard of me, and maybe some of you haven't. So, let me introduce myself so there is no mistake about who I am and what I am doing here." I pitched my voice so it carried to every ear and every mind present. I looked to the left and saw the two brothers from Hunter's house Diya, Oringo, and Gahjji. With them, I saw the sisters Devana and Dali Okar, but I wasn't expecting to see Holter Wellsley. My brows frowned, but I saw the slight shake of Devana's head, so I held my comment on that one. I looked around but didn't see his brother, and I knew I would have to get that story before we all left this place. The Blue Moon was high in the pitch-black sky, giving us the only light. The fire burned brighter when I spoke as if I was giving it power, or was the moon and fire itself giving me power?

"My name is Taria Cross, and I am the daughter of Joziah Cross. I don't know what you heard or if it was the truth. Before last year I didn't know this world held so many secrets. I did not know my family held so many deadly secrets about this world. I found myself in a world where I was turned into a vampire to save my life. That was all before I knew I was a Hunter. Without even knowing that fact, I was fighting with the principles of what and who a Hunter should be. Yes, I am a vampire, and yes, I am a Hunter. So now that is out of the way, maybe we can understand why this meeting has been called." I said, looking at each person I could catch the eye of. I could feel my father step forward to stand at my side. He stood tall with his hands behind his back. Feet spread apart.

"What my daughter says is all true. Her mother and I kept her from this life when she was born. As we can see, that was not her fate, and as far as her being a vampire, that must have always been her fate."

"How do we know her Hunter's responsibilities will be put first!" Someone yelled from the back.

"If she is the Queen to Michael Vaughn, how do we know that will not interfere in her Hunter duties? How do we know what we discuss regarding vampires that will not be shared?" I looked to my left because of that voice I knew. Holter Wellsley stepped forward with his arms crossed over his chest.

"There is no if about Holter. I am Queen to Michael Vaughn, and worrying over things like this will not help the situation we find ourselves in. I take my responsibilities on each side very seriously. This meeting is about coming together to make this world better. This is about who will be the Hunter they were born to be when the next battle arises. I stand here to tell you that the ways Hunters have followed since the Ryder family took over have been wrong. They lead, and you all follow, even though each house has a say in the matter. Beverly Ryder and her children helped bring that demon everyone saw on this Earth! She worked alongside the Van Allan family to destroy what WE are supposed to protect! Where were all of you when this was happening?" I said, looking around. Shock was written on many faces and disbelief.

"Where was Joziah Cross? He left us without a leader and the rest of the Cross family!" One man in front yelled. I looked at his colors and knew he was from the Diya house.

"Oh, I can answer that question for you," my father growled. "I went to someone who is Royalty in the wolf shifter packs. I was captured and deceived by Beverly, who helped the Van Allan family hold me prisoner for years. Years that I will never get back! They used my knowledge to help bring a powerful demon to this Earth, but my daughter was here, and she stopped it. With me gone, my family targeted Beverly, but I assure you they will come and stand with us." I reached out to my father, trying to ease his tension. His fists were balled, and he stood rigid to the spot.

"We called you here because we need to know who is willing to be the Hunters of old and who will fight in the battles to come for this Earth. There is also another reason we made this call. My father has told you who betrayed him, but he is not saying that Beverly will come to your house if you do not bow down to her. Beverly will make Hunter her personal army to do with what she wants. You all could pass through and be here because you want a change and do what you were born to do. Before we can do what we were blessed with gifts to do, we must fight! Today is the day you decide what side you want to be on! I said this the night of the battle with Amu. You will either ride with Beverly or be a true Hunter!" Everyone talked at once, and some still didn't believe what was said. The only thing that turned the tide was when an indistinct murmur started from the left that repeated four words repeatedly until it took over the entire crowd.

"True Hunters Will Reign, True Hunters, Will Reign, True Hunters Will Reign!" The chanting got louder as each Hunter raised their weapons of choice. I pulled out the twins raising them into the night sky, and the moon blazed brighter as we screamed.

ANGELIC

I got dressed in a long silver backless Parada gown. I finished my makeup in the mirror and watched in my eyes as Angelic screamed for release. "Keep screaming. Jinx will always have control, and I have everything you thought you could steal from me." I smiled and blinked. I pushed Angelic in the back of my thoughts and waved a hand in front of the mirror. I didn't have a lot of time once I used this spell. Naki was strong and could get ahold of Jason's panther quickly.

"Jinx, is everything a go?" Masika hissed. She looked worse than the last time I saw her.

"Yes! Are you sure you will be able to handle this? You don't look—"

"Don't worry about me. Just get it done. I will be here and waiting." I fixed my lips one last time before nodding.

"Be ready because I cannot hold this portal for long."

"Why can't I just come through?" Masika asked for the second time.

"Because this house is warded up the ass. The only ones who could create a portal on this land are the blood owners of it." I snapped. "Just be ready for your gift!" I waved a hand and turned for the door. I sprinted through the house, making it to the back of the property. I could smell the newly becoming shifter, leading me to a house. When I started for the step, I felt a shocking sensation run through my body. "Shit!" I said, stepping back. I looked up and around and saw the warding for demons and witches. Taking a deep breath, the scent of a Hunter hit my nose. Hunter's blood was spilled around this place, forming a warding circle to ward off evil. I let a low growl slip through my lips. Before I could stop it, I could feel Angelic pulling herself forward.

"It is a new time now, Jinx. This will not last much longer, even if I have to die to get rid of you," she whispered.

I stepped away from the building and shoved her consciousness back down. I had to change strategies, so I moved back where I could feel and smell the panther and elf the strongest. I knew I would have to be quick because doing this spell without placing the hair on him would only last but so long. I opened the paper that held a few strands of hair I picked up off the table where he had lain. I whispered the words of awakening and pain.

"Hear my words and raise feel the pain of death. Feel the burning fires of hell flow through your veins. Raise and attack until you feel no more pain." I repeated the words as I swayed in the evening breeze. I repeated the words until the first scream filled the night. I stopped and smiled as I made my way back to the house. Let the chaos begin.

Chapter Seventeen

LaToya

I closed my eyes and let the pages of my grimoire filter through my mind. There was much text and spells written, but what fucked with me were the black spots.

"Damn it!" I said, opening my eyes once more. We were still driving but would visit close to the first pack. There was a lot that Quinn had to do to build relationships with these shifters and figure out what help they needed if any.

"What are you trying to do?" Quinn asked while looking both ways before he made the left turn.

"I was looking over my grimoire again, but these black spots keep showing up, and every time I ask Rhonda about it, she changes the subject."

"Well, maybe that's because your short ass shouldn't be messing around with it. Your mother and the book are trying to protect you." He said, making too much damn sense.

"Protect me from what? Hell, I should know about everything so I can protect myself and my family." I grumbled. Quinn said nothing, so I turned to face him. He looked straight ahead, but his warm hand rested on my thigh. He squeezed it before opening his mouth.

"I know you can handle yourself and that you took to being a Witch like a bad bitch—" I smirked at him, and he shook his head. "But some things aren't to be messed with. Knowing more about your kind and your powers will help you learn what you need to. Don't rush into something you know nothing about, babe." As usual, I said nothing because he made perfect sense, so I sighed and closed my eyes again.

This time I would shine a light in those empty black spots and discover what was hidden from me. I knew Quinn had a point, but why shouldn't I know if it's a part of my family's grimoire?

I didn't know how long my eyes were closed, but they snapped open when I heard my name.

"LaToya! Are you good, babe? I have been shaking you for five minutes," Quinn said with worry. I heard the babies in the back waking, knowing they would have to eat soon.

"My bad, I must have dozed off. Are we here?" I said, stretching.

"Yeah, we are staying outside of the pack lands for tonight. We are stopping at this motel until the morning." I looked into his dark eyes and saw he was worried as hell about me.

"Ok. I'm good, babes, believe me. I am just tired of that all. Let's settle the babies and talk about our next move." I said, pushing him gently out of the way so I could get out of the truck. I stood up and looked around, seeing everyone doing the same. I saw my mother jump out of the van she drove that had my grandparents in it. She walked over toward us as Quinn removed our belongings.

"Hey, mom. What's up?" I asked, turning to check on the twins.

"Nothing. I am going to get a few of the wolves to help with your mama and pop. Then I am going to bed. Do you need help with my grandbabies?" She asked, looking at them over my shoulder.

"Naw, we will be fine. Get them settled and get some rest." She kissed me and then each baby before taking my advice. I blinked a few times as a feeling of darkness filled my veins. The coldness tried to creep into my organs, but I pushed it back with force. I jumped up, looking my body over, hoping I wasn't being attacked again, but I saw nothing. I shook my head and reached in for a car seat.

"I got the other one," Quinn said, opening the other door.

We got into the room, where I got the babies changed and fed. After we got Riaan fed, bathed, and to sleep, I put the weird feeling out of my mind.

"I think I am going to join them after I feed Reign," I said with a laugh.

"Aight, well, I am going to go and run with a few members of the pack. Get a lay of the land. See what we can pick up." Quinn said while he took his shirt off. I watched as he began taking off his clothes while I continued to feed the baby. He looked up once his jeans were down, probably noticing I hadn't said anything. "What?" He asked, looking at me like I was crazy.

"I don't know why you stopped because I was damn sure enjoying watching your fine ass strip for me." I smiled. He kicked off his jeans and smirked at me. I watched his hard chest and equally rock-hard abs flex as he removed the rest of his clothes. I let my eyes travel down his body and back to his face. He watched me watch him, and the sexy-as-hell smile told me he knew exactly what I was thinking.

"If you are asleep when I get back, don't worry. I will make sure you wake up." He licked his thick lips, and I bit down on my tongue. He shifted before I knew it, and I got up to open the door. Holding Reign to my chest, I watched him and the other dash off into the trees.

"Shit," I whispered because I swear his ass got sexier every damn day. I could feel the slickness between my legs and had to ignore it.

After getting out of the shower, I looked in the mirror and almost screamed. I couldn't tell if I was asleep and dreaming or if this shit was real. I watched in horror as a woman lay on a bed stretched out, looking like something was taking control of her body. Her screams and how her body twisted had my body feeling her pain.

"NO! NO! I won't let you have him! NO!" She screamed. I looked around frantically, trying to figure out how to help her when the image changed, and the screaming woman stood before me. She was in the mirror, but I didn't think she noticed me. I watched as she put on her make-up in a bathroom that looked so familiar.

"I have to be trippin. This... what the hell—" I saw her mouth move, but I couldn't make out the words, and then she turned and left. The image blurred, and I was staring at myself once again. "What the fuck?" I whispered. I started feeling that creepy feeling again, but a waspy voice echoed in my thoughts.

"You have read the dark pages of your ancestors. Knowledge is available, but this magic comes with a price." I closed my eyes, trying to force myself to wake up. I had to be tripping hard. I was tired and drained from today and last night.

"The cost is power. So many things I can show you with mirror magic. So many things you might want to see."

"Naw, I am good. Whatever the hell you are, you can take this shit back. I don't need it." I said into the empty space. I shook my head and wished I had listened to Quinn.

"Are you sure?" The mirror moved once more, and I closed my eyes. I reached down and picked up my towel. I hadn't realized I had dropped. "Look, look, look, LOOK!" The voice screamed the last word, and I opened my eyes only to see the woman shove Garrett into the mirror.

"NO!" I screamed as my eyes rolled into the back of my head.

BEVERLY

Jinx's plan was good because having Taria's child would bring her right to me. Naki, the grandmother she is, will try to come with her, but how will she choose which child to save? I didn't have a problem with the wolf children like the others, but the little boy will make good bate. Having him will drive Joziah to rush to save him, but having him be distracted by his precocious Hunters attacking law-abiding citizens will give him pause. Whatever Hunter I lose in the process is one step closer to being on top. The spell Apu and his Druids had given me had been sown deep in the veins of the Hunters. I could sway to my side. Every order I give will be followed even if that means they will die to the full fill it.

I turned, hearing quiet footsteps behind me to see my son Zareh.

"Yes?" I asked, spinning around.

"We are ready, and I have the Hunters in place at the hotel owned by Michael and Taria." It was dumb luck that I had some pull around the city as a council member's wife. When I heard about the purchase, I had my Hunter in place before the ward was placed around it. Having the Druids wipe their minds and implant a timer was genius on my part. They won't know what hit them. Government officials and Senators that joined the uppity Blue Blood bitches were in for a surprise. Nothing was safe, and there was no guarantee for anyone. Joziah will run to protect the innocent, leaving me time to kill his daughter and give her body and soul to Apu. Then I will have what I want, and Joziah will bow at my feet as ruling Hunter and be all mine.

"Good. I want you and your sister outside of the hotel. When he makes a scene showing these people, they are unsafe. Take a few other Hunters with you. Have them attacked when Joziah shows up. Wear our House crest and show them we are the only ones to save them."

"Yes, mother." He said with no inflection. I looked into his eyes and hated to see the glazed look, but he wasn't his sister. I had to use the spell on my son, but he will soon see that I am right and we should rule. I heard Jamari and Arawn Wellsley coming into the room.

"Jamari, look after your brother and make sure nothing goes wrong. Arawn, have you found your brother yet?" I was sure his brother didn't have the stomach or heart for this, and I would kill him if he did come back.

"No, ma'am. I will find him, and he will be a part of this." I nodded.

"Fine. Now dress some of the Hunters in the Cross-house crest and be sure they are caught killing or hurting a bystander. They can die, or you can choose to save them but make it look good and make Joziah look like he is the villain." I wave my hand to send them out. I turned back to the large mirror, waiting for my gift to be sent through.

Michael

I saw the surprise and then the sadness on my uncle's face. Camron and Marcus looked so much like their father that if his hair didn't have strands of white, you would think he was one of them.

"She will be joining us in a little while. You must understand how hard this will be for her. She has to sit on the council where her mother will be brought up on charges. She just wanted a little more time and will be here." His answers made perfect sense to me, but the feeling in my soul and blood told me something wasn't right, but I didn't know what it was.

"You sent the car back for her?" I asked as I watched my mother make her way over toward us.

"Yes, of course. She also wants time to get herself together. She is of mind to think my sister doesn't trust her." Caleb said as my mother approached.

"That is simply true, brother. I am sorry, but things haven't been adding up for a while now. I wanted to say something to you, but—" Her words trailed off.

"She is your best friend, Katherine. I don't understand why you would think we would betray you this way." He said, shaking his head. I looked around, but we kept it low enough normal people wouldn't hear, but other ears were listening. I caught the gaze of Camila, and she came over. Her arm was wrapped around a man I hadn't seen in a while, and one I thought could be behind the whole attempt on Taria's life.

"I thought you might want to use the room toward the left to prepare for the upcoming events." Camila smiled. I could see the tension in her eyes and her quick side-eye of her father.

"Yes, thank you, Camila. You have done a wonderful job tonight. Erik, thank you for being here. I know this will be hard because this is a Blue Blood." I said as I reached out for his offered hand.

"Yes, this is awful, but it has to be done. We are also here about your crowning and to meet you... your Hunter Queen. That should be interesting. Where is she, by the way?" He said, looking around as if he would spot her.

"Father, we have time for that later." Camila chuckled softly. Looking my mother over before letting Camila go and taking my mother into his arms, he pivoted.

"I am so happy to see you, my Queen. I always hoped–" His cultured voice deepened, and I could hear the true affection in it. Just because of that show of emotion for my mother, I knew he at least couldn't be a part of the bullshit.

My mother and Erik Augustine pulled apart, and she assured him they would speak soon. My uncle, mother, and I moved to the private office off the side. Before I had the door fully closed, Caleb started once again.

"I don't know what happened between you two. The day Gio turned her, you pulled away. I thought you were happy. I found my Kindred just as you found yours?" I watched as Caleb threw up his hands like he had had this conversation many times before. I remember back, and I never saw any hostility between them.

"Kindred! She is not your Kindred, Caleb. I don't know what she is, but everything changed that day! She wasn't the same, and I don't know why you can't see that!" My uncle moved swiftly, and the anger on his face made me move to stand next to my mother. She held out a hand, telling me to be still.

"I think I know if she wasn't my Kindred. She is the woman I fell in love with all those years ago. How can you not see that?" He growled.

Caleb was always laid back and never seemed threatening, but people forget he was my father's right hand. He was his shadow in the night or blade of the throne. He was deadly, just like his sons. I watched as my mother stood tall. Her skin glowed with an inner light Cam always said she had. She moved to stand toe to toe with her brother, looking up into his dark, almost midnight-black eyes.

"If that is true, why didn't you both look for me? Why was my son with those people? She didn't even like her family, Caleb. Why would she think it was ok for Michael to stay with them? Why, if she is the woman and best friend that I knew, aren't you wearing the charm that was given to her by Jaser Cross? I thought I saw things when I first saw you two, but I wasn't. You know her gifts are called to demons or dark Witches. How long has she not had that charm on Caleb? The day I finally realized it wasn't on her body was the night we were attacked. Tell me why you can't see what I see plain as day?" The room was silent until a buzzing started in my pocket. I pulled out my phone, seeing it was Cam, and sent it to voicemail. I would get back to him later because I could answer one of those questions.

"Mother, I told uncle Caleb I would stay with Victor and Martin. He didn't just leave me there." I said through gritted teeth. If I had thought right, I would never have left with them. None of this would have ever happened, but was that a good or bad thing? Or was it just fate?

"Yes, Michael, I understand that, but," Mother said, still not taking her eyes from Caleb. He sucked in a breath and finished her sentence in that weird-ass twin way of theirs.

"But the promise and bond I made with my sister were always to save her children, no matter the case. To take care of her children if she could no longer." He looked into her eyes again, and I saw the dawning and anger fill them. "They did something to me, Katherine, but I still don't believe Angelic had anything to do with it." My phone buzzed again, but the knock on the door had all three of us turn to see who it could be. I reached out, opened the door, and saw Douglas Walton. His burnt orange colored eyes bore into mine before he bowed.

"It is time." Things still weren't adding up, and something was off. I could feel it. When Taria returns to this realm, I think I will be clearer-minded. One thing that was for sure was that Angelic still wasn't present for the trial and sentencing of her mother.

"Let's make this quick," I growled, and he turned to lead us into the grand ballroom.

Chapter Eighteen

GARRETT

I opened my eyes to see Lily and grandma looking down at me. I was trying to dream or see whatever it was that I was feeling. Something was wrong, but I couldn't figure it out. I wanted to help dad because he could see what it was. I just wanted to keep my mom and Lily safe. "Garr... can you watch a movie with me?" Lily smiled. She was in her pajamas, and I could smell that she had just had a bath because she smelled like a girl. She smelled like bubble gum and sugar.

"Sure, as long as it's not Disney," I said, sitting up.

"Ok, Lily, I want you to listen to Garrett while I take my bath, and then I will sit with you two and finish the movie until your mom gets home," Grandma said. Lily nodded and slid down her body to throw herself onto my bed.

"You can pick the movie, Garrett." She laughed. I went over to the Tv to turn it on when a loud roar made Lily scream.

"It's going to eat me!" Lily screamed, jumping out of bed to run to grandma.

"Lily, I want you to stay here with Garrett, and do not leave this room until an adult comes to get you. I don't care what you two hear. Do not leave this room!" She looked at me, making sure I understood. Poppa said that I was the man of the house right now, so I had to protect my sister.

"Yes, ma'am." I nodded and reached out for Lily. Grandma turned and ran out of the door, closing it behind her. The roar got louder, and so did the screaming. I knew that it would all be ok because grandma was strong, and she would never let anything happen. Plus, we still had shifters here.

"Garrett, this is what happened. This is my dream." Lily cried, and I had to do something to fix it.

"It will be ok, Lily. Mommy, daddy, both grandmas, and poppa would never let anything hurt us." I said while pulling her away from the door. I turned on the Tv and looked for anything that would distract her.

"But Garrett, I know the monster wants me, and the monster wants you too." I looked back at her words when there was a knock on my door. It opened, and Aunt Angelic stood there with a frown.

"Garrett, I need your help. Your grandmother wants some healing potions I have, but I have to go and meet your father. Can you run them to her? I know you are a big boy, right? I looked at her like she was tripping because I wasn't five.

"She told me to stay with Lily," I said, finding some dumb show Lily liked. Another scream and roaring hit the air making Lily jump. I hit play and turned up the sound.

"Yes, I know, but this is important, and you can come right back." I could hear the screaming and knew this was bad. Someone needed help, and I could help them. I was leaving with an adult, and I would be only a few minutes. I looked back, seeing her standing right outside the door, making a hurry-up motion. I turned back to Lily.

"Lillian, I want you to listen to me. I will be right back. I'm going to help out real quick." I said, putting on my shoes.

"No, Garrett. What if..."

"Lily, I will be right back, don't worry. I'm bigger than you. I can protect myself." I said. I rubbed her head and went to help. When I crossed the threshold, I could tell I was already too late. I saw when Angelic made a waving motion to close the door to my room. I felt it when she grabbed my arm and dug her nail in. I tried to fight like uncle Marcus and Camron showed me, but it was too late. My body went weak, and my legs stopped working. I could see Angelic picking me up by my arm and dragging me across the floor. My eyes were staring at the ceiling, but I could move them, and when she looked down, I could see I was going to die in her eyes.

I tried to kick or scream, but I couldn't do anything. No one was around or in the house to see this woman taking me. Why did I leave my room and leave Lily? I knew better, and now I can't protect my sister or see my new baby sister. We made it to her room, and she pulled me up and faced me toward the mirror. She waved her hand, and the glass moved, and when it did, I could see the ghost in her eyes crying out to me.

"This gift is for you, Masika," she sneered and tossed me through the portal in the mirror.

Lily

I looked back at the TV when the door closed. I was unhappy that Garrett left, but I knew this would happen. I jumped off of Garrett's bed and got on my knees to look under it. I knew the monster was coming, and I was supposed to hide. I already knew that wasn't going to stop this monster. I pulled out my pink teddy bear backpack that daddy gave me and put it on. I waited beside the bed, looking at the door and knowing that if I didn't leave with the monster, I would never be able to help the man with the rainbow eyes.

I jumped when the door crashed open and saw that lady standing there. She took Garrett, but he wasn't with her.

"Lily, come with me. Something has happened to Garrett." I wanted to cry because I knew something really had happened to Garrett. I didn't know if I was a big girl enough to do this, so I shook my head no.

"Mommy said never to leave with a stranger," I whispered. I saw her eyes burn bright, so I knew she was mad. I shook because I wanted Garrett and daddy. I wanted my mommy and aunt, Toya.

"I said, come here right now, Lily. I am your aunt, Angelic. Your uncle Camron's mother," she growled. I watched as her fangs grew, like when mommy was mad.

"No," I cried. She was so mad, but she smiled at me just before she really got mad.

"Do you like flowers? If I make you a pink flower, can we go and help Garrett?" She asked. I was still crying, but I nodded yes. The rainbow-eyed man was always upset because he couldn't grow things anymore. Someone took his gift. I wiped my eyes as she whispered and opened her hand to show me a glowing pink flower. I moved closer, trying to see the other colors in the middle. I was closer to the door, and she stepped back.

"It's so pretty," I whispered, taking another step.

"I can make you more, but we need to hurry."

"To save Garrett?" I asked because she couldn't be the monster if she could make pretty flowers.

"Yes," she smiled again. I moved quickly and reached for the flower. Before I could touch it, the pretty pink flower dried up and turned brown. It crumbled just as I reached her, and her smile was gone. I tried to run as uncle Marcus told me if I was scared, but she caught me. When I turned to look at her, she was different. She was just like the flower dried up and brown. She was the monster I saw in my dreams.

Taria

As we left the meeting, I thought things would go well. The ones who spoke up let it be known that Beverly and her people were also trying to gather Hunters to their side. Some from the house present followed her, but others had concerns that the choice was real. We all knew that a war was coming between Hunters, and none of us wanted it. I spoke to Holter, and he told me about his brother. He seemed hurt and honestly out of sorts about the whole thing.

"Taria, it's time to go back." My father said after speaking with Joshua. I always thought my father was the only child, but apparently, papa was a rolling stone. I knew one day I would have to get the full story about my father and my family. So many things I didn't know and too many secrets to uncover.

"It was nice to meet you, Uncle Josh," I smiled. His smile said it all because I could tell he was a Hunter, but he lacked the power my father and I possessed.

"I am so happy to meet you, Taria," he said, pulling me into a hug. Letting him go, I looked at my cousin Jayla and smiled. I had more family when I only thought I had my parents and Toya.

"I am so glad I met you, Taria. We will come and see you and uncle Joziah soon," she smiled, and I could see it as well. She was a fighter, don't get me wrong but not a demon Hunter. She was a dark brown complexion with the most gorgeous turquoise eyes I had ever seen. She was tall, at least 5'11, and athletic, but I could tell she would rather not fight but teach or learn. They were not like my father and me. Now I see why they wanted my father and me dead. We closed the gates of hell because they knew we would be here to shove their asses back where they came from if they tried.

"I can't wait!" I waved and followed my father to the trees where we last saw Beverly. Just as we came, the trees parted for us to return the way we came, and the moon burned hotter than the sun ever felt. I could feel the energy and power filling while I was here. It was high I had never felt, and I understood why my father said staying too long could have you trapped.

"Are you ready, baby girl?" I nodded and watched as he opened the gateway to head back home.

It felt like a light went off when I stepped forward. We hit the ground and landed on our feet in the cool night's air. It took a minute before things caught up to me, and when they did, my blood ran cold. My father and I turned as one when we heard the screaming coming in the house's direction. I moved, not checking to see if my father was following. I had a terrible feeling something was wrong, and the turning in my stomach worsened as I grew closer.

I passed by Leila, sitting beside a large black panther that was sleeping in her lap, and had no time to ask questions. The screaming turned into growls and roars as I crashed through the back doors of the house.

"Garrett! Lily! Garrett! Lily!" My mother roared. I took in her direction, my heart slamming in my chest. I could feel the tears stinging my eyes at the sheer panic in my mother's voice.

"Mom!" I growled, and I knew my eyes were glowing brightly. She turned in circles while in her third form. She spun around, growling, and charged at me until she realized who I was.

"Taria?" Her voice was distorted until she shifted back into her human form. "They are gone." She cried and fell to her knee. The sharp pain that was grazing my heart stabbed it all the way through, and I lost me got a damn mind.

"Where the fuck are my children!" I felt more than see my father move past me to my mother, who was sobbing uncontrollably. I turned, taking in every damn scent in the house. I could feel the storm moving my way as lightning danced in my veins.

"That bitch took them! Her scent was the last by Garrett's door." My mother said with a growl. I snapped my head toward her, just noticing her crying had stopped. She stood and pulled away from my father. Her eyes glowed a bright yellow as she walked toward me.

"Who?" I was shaking and thought I had an idea, but should she be with Michael and Katherine?

"Angelic." My mother spat. The house shook, and I could hear the whimpers from the shifters in the distance. I turned, moving through the house to find her scent. I stopped outside Garrett's door and kept moving. I tore into their room and felt the ward she tried to place break. The smell in the room was bitter and smelled of something rotten. It was coming from the bathroom. I walked in and looked around, and stopped. I moved closer to the mirror, where a drop of blood was smuggled into it.

"Garrett's blood," I whispered. I pulled out my phone to call Michael, but Quinn's number flashed across the screen before dialing.

"I can't talk." My voice broke, and my tears slid down my face.

"It's Toya." Her voice was raspy, and she sounded as if she was in pain.

"They took my kids, Toya!" I screamed. I punched the mirror in front of me. I knew it had something to do with why my babies were gone.

"I know! I have been trying to call everyone for hours. That bitch whoever she was throwing Garrett into the mirror. I saw it, and I couldn't do a fucking thing!"

"What did she look like?" As Toya gave me the description of the bitch, her death warrant was signed. "Taria, can you hear me?" Toya screamed into the phone.

"Yeah, yeah, I'm listening." I wiped my eyes and pulled myself together.

"Lily was not with him. I don't know where she is, but I can get you to Garrett if you go now. I can follow where that portal went but I can't join you. My power will be maximized with this one," she said.

"It's ok. Just get me there so I can bring him home," I said through clenched teeth.

"Hung up and go through when that mirror begins to move. It won't last long." She said, panting.

"I got this," I said, hanging up the phone. I turned to my mother.

"Find Lily. Call Michael. I have to get my son." The words burned my throat because a mother wants to choose between her children. I knew where Garrett could be and had to take that chance. I had no idea where Lily was, but I knew Michael would burn this world to the ground to find her.

"I am coming with you," I argued when she held up a hand. "This was my fault. Joziah, find our granddaughter and get to Michael." I swallowed hard, hating I had to leave without knowing where my baby girl was. My stomach flipped again when I saw the mirror move. I felt my mother by my side.

"Both of you return, and I will have our Lily here waiting. Taria, you know the demon is involved. This is what we do, Taria. You got this." I nodded and turned back to the mirror as it turned into a silver liquid, and I jumped through.

Chapter Nineteen

MICHAEL

We didn't allow the government officials to join the trial meeting, but they will be here to witness the crowning ceremony. I followed Douglas and Camila to the room where Sara was being held. I looked behind me, seeing my mother follow Caleb.

"Caleb, I would ask if you would wait with the other Blue Bloods. Also, please make sure Angelic is on her way. We will start in ten minutes." I said, turning back around because I wasn't asking. It was an order.

"Yes." His voice rumbled with irritation. I could feel his emotions were all over the place, and I could tell he was questioning everything he had ever known about his Kindred. He turned, and I walked inside the room with my mother and Douglas. My phone began to buzz again, but I ignored it.

"Sara, if you want any lenience, you need to tell us who else is trying to hurt the Queen?" I said, standing in front of her. She sat on a chair, and I could tell traces of the poison still ran through her veins, but it wasn't enough to kill her. I saw her eyes flick to mine, and the hatred that burned there made me smile. I smiled because not only was there hatred but fear as well. I could tell it was hard for her to speak, and I didn't give a shit. I wouldn't even try to help someone standing by while her family planned to take over the Earth, but time was short.

"I will not give you much but enough for you to speak. Believe me, if you do not, your pain will be nothing compared to me breaking your mind." I would do it knowing it took a lot of energy and power. Yes, I was full of the power Gio passed on, but it wasn't always at my back and call just yet. I rubbed my thumbnail across my finger, but before I would reach out, my mother caught my arm.

"I will give her my blood." She said while staring holes into the side of her head. I saw Sara's eyes widen as she realized who had spoken. My mother moved so Sara could see her clearly, and the smell of fear filled the room. I watched as my mother bit her lip and wiped a bead of blood that weld up onto her thumb across her mouth. I could tell Sara was doing her best to move, but she could do nothing. It was fast when Katherine reached out, pushing Sara's lips apart, and rubbed her blood along her tongue.

"Your blood is too pure to let her have even a drop of it." My mother growled. I watched as Sara's mouth began to move, her fangs descended, and her eyes began to glow.

"Douglas! You are a fucking trader to your family!" She growled as she tried to avoid my eyes and my mother's. I didn't know the full scope of my mother's powers, but I knew what she held was tremendous. Katherine stood back up to her full height, and the platinum gold crown with one deep red ruby in the center made her whole stance regal.

"I didn't ask you to speak to Douglas. He has made his choices." I growled.

"Where is my daughter? I claim Blue Bloods, right!" She demanded. I knew that she would, and that was ok. I wanted to snap her fucking neck for the part she played in my family's hardships and for Taria being the target of her sick sons. I had to play this right and show everyone that I wouldn't rule by brutality, but I wasn't going to be anyone's bitch either.

She tried to muster up saliva to spit at my feet, but out of the corner of my eye, I saw my mother raise her hand and close it into a fist. Sara's head lifted with the motion, and her mouth slammed tight.

"That is right, Sara, but you will not speak unless I allow it." My mother growled. I could see the pain and anger glinting in her eyes. I knew she was thinking about my father and what Victor had done to her for so long.

"Douglas, find Camila and let her know we are ready. Sara will be contained, and they can give her the antidote before they bring her in." I commanded.

"I got you, my King." He said with a slight bowing. He disappeared as my phone began to buzz once more. I pulled it out of my pocket, thinking it may be Taria since I felt my heartbeat again. I looked at the number, and it was her father.

"Joziah? What's up? Where is Taria?" I asked as ice filled my veins when I felt the short connection I had just had with her snap. I could hear the creak on the phone, and I knew I had to loosen my grip before I broke it.

"The children are missing, and... and we think it was Angelic." I felt the building shake, and everything in my vision burned gold. I could barely hear the rest of what he was saying until I felt my mother's hand on my arm. I knew she heard what the fuck was going on, and so did Sara because her laugh snapped me out of it.

"What the fuck did you just say?" My voice was like ice, and I knew it was true because the room temperature dropped, allowing me to see my breath.

"Taria has gone for Garrett, and I am tracking Lily. I am headed your way." The phone was disconnected, but I didn't care. My mother reached out and swiped her hand across the air knocking Sara unconscious. My phone buzzed once, making me look down. I had twenty-two missed calls, and they were all from Cam. I turned for the door as I dialed because I had to find my little girl and kill Angelic for touching my children. I had no idea how she did it or why, but for damn sure, I was going to find out.

"Mike! What the fuck? I have been—"

"Gone. Your mother took my fucking children." I growled as the door flew off its hinges. Outside the door stood Camila with wide eyes and Caleb and the other head council members.

"That is why I have been calling! I found out some shit down here in Florida, and my mother was part of everything all along! I… I'm unsure if I can even trust my father right now." I saw Caleb's eye widen at the comment and the other Blue Bloods' stiffen at what news they heard. My eyes locked onto his as his phone slipped from his ear, and he shook his head. With one move, I held Caleb off the ground slamming him into the wall. The granite cracked at the force as my hand tightened around his throat. Every memory I had filled my mind, and I could wrap my head around my own blood doing this. Who else was next? It started with Damon and now my uncle. Who in my family could I trust? I could feel his struggle, but I held him still, and everyone around me knew that shit couldn't have been easy. He was the warrior of our kind, the one who trained every Blue Blood to be the fighter they are, but I was King. Everyone will understand if I didn't want you to fucking move, you won't. With one hand, I brought the tall vampire face to face. I could see the golden light reflecting off of her dark skin.

"Tell. Me. Where. My. Children. Are." Every word was growled. It came deep into the back of my throat. I saw in his eyes and his mind the confusion. I didn't give two shits as I tore through his mind looking for answers. I dropped him, letting his body hit the ground, and turned to the rest of these mother fuckers. I would rip every mind apart until I found my child. Everyone in my line of sight started to take a stance readying themselves for a fight they would lose, when an explosion sounded outside.

Joziah

The ground shook, and I knew I was close to the hotel. I didn't have to say another word because I was close. I was close enough to see reporters lined up outside, waiting for the next high-profile person to enter the door. I followed the trial Angelic because of the small energy signals left by Lily. I smiled because she would, in time, make a great Hunter and, most likely, more. To be so young, she was smart as a whip, so that was why I couldn't understand why she would leave Garrett's room. Her trial stopped as if she had completely left this Earth. I started to turn when I saw a tall man step out from the crowd of reporters and bystanders who just wanted to see something supernatural.

I was wild because times have changed since the last time humans started to believe. Most would run and hide in their homes. They would fall to their knees in prayer, thinking every supernatural was a demon coming to claim their souls. I shook away a million memories as the crest the man wore on his jacket glowed at night. A dark red circle with a sword in the middle with two snakes called the Inland taipan intertwining around the blade. I looked around because that was the crest of House Ryder, and Beverly could be near. The Ryder house specialty kills using their blades' tips coated in the snake's venom. The venom also harmed most supernaturals because of how fast it was killed. The paralyzing venom causes hemorrhaging in blood vessels and muscle tissues, making it almost impossible to heal immediately. When he lifted his head, I was no more than twenty feet away from him now, trying to move people out of the way. The man was tall and fair-skinned with light brown hair, but his eyes were so dull they looked lifeless. Hell pulled out his sword, and the people around him began to move as the murmuring became louder.

"You don't have to do this!" I yelled as I reached for a blade on my vest. I didn't have time for this. I had to find Lily and the bitch that took her.

"Cross Hunters will reign supreme!" He screamed and turned, slicing his sword and cutting off a cameraman's arm. I threw the blade I held, hitting the Hunter in the forehead, dropping him where he stood. The screaming started, and another Hunter stepped forward wearing a vest like mine. The moon with flames surrounding it. It was a cheap and pale imitation, but I saw right through the bullshit.

"Cross Hunter..." She started to scream, but my next blade found a home in her throat. That's when I saw Jamari and Zareh attacking anyone who got in their way as they headed for me.

"Joziah Cross, father of Taria Cross, we are here to stop your power rise. We will protect these humans from a bloodthirsty vampire and her rouge father!" Jamari screamed and then charged me.

It seemed that Beverly didn't care much about her children if she sent these young Hunters to their deaths. I moved while Jamari and another redhead, Hunter, came charging forward. It was as if they moved in slow motion to me. I made it to the cameraman that lost his arm, and I wrapped the stump and whispered healing words to give him a chance of survival. I looked down at the camera that was still running. I didn't know if it was running a live feed or being filmed for a later news feed. Whatever the case, it didn't matter because it would work in my favor. It wasn't the large cameras I was used to seeing before I was kidnapped but small and sleek. The reporter that was with the cameraman was moving to help him. In three seconds, she would be close enough.

I stopped moving and held the cameraman gently, laying him on the ground as the reporter fell to her knees. With my other hand, I picked up the camera handing it to her as she stared at the man who was now sleeping.

"He is healing. He will survive, but you must film this story. His red lips opened, but I was almost out of time. "You film so his attackers can be brought to justice, but that is what a true Cross Hunter stands for. I will protect you but film everything." She blinked fast but accepted the camera with numb fingers, but I saw her instinct for a story kick in.

I turned just in time as two-bladed came crashing down. I had pulled my katana from my back, blocking one swing from Jamari, and used my throwing blade to cut the hand of the other Hunter. When his hand fell to the ground and his blood hit the air, I knew it was a Wellsley Hunter, and this was Arawn, the older brother of Holter.

"Your mother was too afraid to face me herself?" I said, pushing Jamari back and dropping low to sidekick Arawn in the leg, making him fall forward as he screamed. He was good because he caught himself as he tied off his hand. I stood back up and swung my katana in an arc, making Jamari retreat further.

"House Ryder will never be afraid of anyone. Look around, Joziah. It's over for you and your blood-sucking daughter. This world will belong to the true Hunter family."

"Is that right?" I said, turning as another Hunter with a fake Cross crest attacked me. I spun as I threw my blade in Arawn's direction, using my fist to backhand the Hunter to the ground. Something was wrong with some of these Hunters. Their eyes weren't right, but there was no time to investigate.

"All Hunters were put here to protect every living being, or have your mother taught you anything?" I said, pushing a human woman down as I took out my gun to shoot a Hunter that was attacking her. I turned, taking three fast shoots at Jamari when she moved. Dropping my head back in the holster, I moved, taking out six small blades and throwing them behind me while standing and moving the woman and another man closer to the reporter. I heard the blades hit my mark as I spun back to block Jamari. The force behind her blow showed me her intent to kill and also had her close enough. I could see her eyes were clear as day. She wanted this just like her mother.

"She told me you were pathetic. You love these weaker humans and supernaturals. You loved them enough to sleep with the one who tried to kill my mother. Once you and your daughter are taken care of, humans will know who is on top, and so will every other supernatural." He sneered. She was young and didn't know she was being used to starting a war. Nothing I said would get through to her. I heard Arawn coughing and pulling himself up off the ground. I looked around, seeing more Hunters starting to attack, and Jamari's smile grew. Causing death and chaos was something a demon wanted, and she didn't even know how badly she was being played — neither she nor Beverly.

I looked to my left and heard cars slamming on breaks and doors opening. I didn't take my eyes off Jamari, but I moved so quickly that Arawn didn't see me pull out my gun as he came up behind me. I let one shot go and dropped my gun from where it was placed. I heard the body hit the ground as footsteps came closer.

"Joziah! What the hell—" I could tell that the two sisters Taria was fond of had arrived.

"Save who you can, and for those who are too far gone, do what you must," I said without turning. More screams came to the right of me as Zareh helped up a steel bar with a button flashing red. "Stop him!" I yelled as I moved to help shield, which I could. Jamari smiled as she turned to push women and men toward what I knew was a bomb.

"Everyone down!" I screamed as I watched Zareh, with his lifeless, dull eyes, press the button that may kill hundreds.

Chapter Twenty

TARIA

After landing on solid ground, I started moving. The dizziness and feeling I was starting to associate with portal jumping didn't hold me back. I felt my mother behind me as we moved through a large empty Mansion. As we moved, I could feel that we were not in Maryland. Hell, we were not on the same plane as the rest of my family.

"They are here." I heard my mother say. I flicked my eyes to the side, seeing that she was partially shifted, and her panther fangs were growing long as they glistened in the firelight that lit the halls.

"Who? Garrett?" I asked, sliding to a stop. The Mansion was missing an entire wall, and as far as the eye could see were large green trees and plants. The jungle stretched far and wide. The sky burned bright with a reddish glow as the temperature rose.

"Masika has Garrett and my brother as well. She has Femi." My mother growled. I looked around and spotted what looked like a temple in the distance. My mother could sense her brother, but what I smelled was a demon. There were demons and Druids in that jungle.

"We will save Garrett and Femi. I know they are there in that temple in the distance because that is exactly where Apu would want his sacrifice." My mother looked, and a roar left her mouth, and whatever was hiding let out one itself.

"She plays games. This is what my home looked like before I left, but this is just a cheap imitation of the beauty of what I called home." I could hear the hurt in her voice, but she knew this wasn't real. After this was dealt with and I had my babies back, we would free her people.

I turned back to face the sprawling jungle and knew whatever lay between my son and me would die. I reached behind me, pulling out both blades to see the moon crest glow with power, and I looked down to see the crest on my shirt shine like a beacon. The light of the moon made a direct beam straight to the temple. I was sure that is where Garrett was being held because he was a Cross as well, and I knew on some level the crest only seeks out our blood.

"Let's go," I growled as the storm in my blood began to build. I jumped from the cliff the Mansion sat on, heading for the jungle floor to get my son.

We hit the ground running, and I already could feel the Druids and demon-possessed Hunters coming at us. Hunters were made of strong shit, and possessing a Hunter or a spell would take a lot of mental abuse. As they started to come at us, I noticed my mother shift into the form she took when we fought at the house. It had to be that some of these Hunters didn't volunteer for this, and I didn't want to hurt them. Even though every bone and cell in my body wanted to kill them, I knew I couldn't because, in the end, I was put here to save everyone, not just those I loved.

"Try not to kill the Hunters!" I said and leaped into the air. I held both blades on my head as I came down in the middle of four Druids and two Hunters. I used an elbow to knock one of the Hunters on the side of the head as I kicked the other into a tree covered in vines were moving. The Druids turned as one holding their hands together, forming black balls of energy to blast my way. I didn't give them two fucking seconds to finish before I moved. The hilt of my swords held a pointy lip, making it easy for me to prick my finger. The blood flowed easily through the sword now as I jammed one into the stomach of Druid and cut off another's head. I knew that one would be back one of these days, but not now. The one who hung on my blade screamed and hissed as my blood burned its insides.

"You can't stop us! You will never stop my master!" It hissed. Using my other sword since the first Druid's body was down, I threw it into another Druid, pinning it to a tree. Taking my now free hand, I placed it on the Druid's head, and the cloak that covered its face fell back. The twisted and mutilated flesh gave me pause at its ugliness but not anymore. I began to whisper as the roars and tears from my mother filled the air. The sky began to turn a deep crimson, but the flashing lightning in my eyes lit the jungle well.

"No! No! Just kill me!" It hissed as the black substance began to flow out of every hole on its body. I felt its boney fingers grip my wrist, but something made the hand desecrate at a touch. I dropped the Druid as it became ash as the first Hunter I hit came crashing into me. I fell to the ground and lost my blade as I held the Hunter away from my body. I had a feeling if they touched my shirt, they would succumb to the same fate the Druid had.

"Cross must die. Cross must die." It repeated over and over. I could hear the other Hunter pulling itself back to her feet, and I knew I didn't have long. I used my strength to lift the Hunter that was on top of me up by the neck as his fingernail dug into the skin on my face.

"Why can't you mother fuckers get a new mantra!" I growled. I knew reaching for the sky wouldn't work because this place wasn't my home, and the storm here could only come from me. The Hunter hissed as it drew blood from my face, and it made me smile just as I summoned the lightning from within to electrocute the fuck out of him. The shock blew him across, slamming him into another Druid behind my mother. I stood with fluid movements picking up my blade just in time to stop the knife coming for my head. I pushed back as I pricked my finger. I punished the Hunter in the face and swiped her legs from under her body. She fell hard to the ground, but that did faze the demon. Its twisted smile died when I leaned over and pressed my bloody hand to her face. I mumbled words that came to me easily, as if I spoke them daily. I watched as their eyes began to bleed black blood, as well as her nose and ears.

"You will never return to another body again," I growled and lifted my hand in the air. The dark black oily substance that was this demon was held to my hand by my blood, and when I closed my hand, it would never return to this plane or any other.

The snap of destroying the Druid and demon caught the attention of the rest. I watched as my mother held a Druid by the head with her massive claws and tore its body in two. The Hunter lay on the ground sucking in air, and tears rolled from her eyes, but I didn't have time for this shit. I moved while pulling out my blade that held one Druid to a tree, and I watched as the vines covered the body while my blood coursed through its veins. I turned to see the other two Druids move back after witnessing the swiftness of what happened to their counterparts.

The rest of the demon-possessed Hunters began to move away, and some opened their mouths as the demons tried to make their escape. They knew if I could get a hold of them, they would never return to fight another fight or steal another soul. I started to move when my mother roared louder than anything. I had never remembered hearing and raising her clawed hands in the air. A bright burst of pearly light shot from her palms, covering us all and making it impossible for a demon to escape into the air. Roars of other panthers came from all around us as I moved. I felt myself doing that light speed I couldn't control. I just knew I had no time for the fuckery. I cut my palm open in one smooth move flinging my blood around and prayed it touched each Druid. I never tried to send a demon back to hell for good and kill a Druid together, but it was the first time for everything.

"End it, Taria!" My mother roared again, making the shield shine with power as it grew strong. I began to speak the words given to my ancestor, Jaser. The word flowed from my lips as everything shined a blind white light, and then there was silence.

LA TOYA

I coughed hard after hanging up with Taria. It took everything out of me to make that portal, but I would do that shit again and again. I could feel Quinn's anger as if it were my own, but I didn't have time for it.

"What the fuck were you thinking? I told you not to mess with that shit, but you never listen!" His growl had the other wolves who came in when they heard me fall to leave the room. I coughed again and pushed myself from the floor, where I had made a hasty circle for the portal.

"Quinn, it wasn't as if I did it on purpose. I'm handling it," I mumbled. I leaned over the sink, looking into the mirror, trying to figure out where the fuck that fake vampire bitch had taken my niece.

"LaToya! Your children were in the other room! That stunt you just pulled was dangerous as fuck. If something is stopping you from seeing it normally, that means stop fucking looking!" He was yelling, but his hands on me were gentle as he rubbed the bruise forming on my hip. I turned around, making him take a step back. I looked up an understanding of what he was saying, but what the fuck was I supposed to do.

"It was from Garrett! She fucking took my niece and nephew, and if it were the twins, I know Taria and Michael would do whatever the fuck was necessary to save them." I felt the tears, and my knees began to shake. My inner magic was drained, and I needed to rest, but I knew deep in my soul that I couldn't. I knew Taria would need me, and I would be there for her just as she was there for me each and every time.

"I know!" He growled as he punched through the wall beside him. I watched as he ran a hand over his face before he spoke. "That isn't the problem, LaToya. The problem is before any of this. You still put yourself in danger. I told you to avoid that darkness, but I know you went looking." His dark brown eyes bored into mine, and I watched as the red ring got brighter. He was right, but if it didn't happen that way, would I have been able to get Taria to where she needed to be?

"Yes, I did, but it had to be for a reason, Quinn. I refuse to be useless when another dark Witch attacks my family or me. I don't care if I have to learn every trick they know. I will not let it consume me." I brushed by him to go into the room to find some clothes. I pulled out some jogging pants and found a tank top and hoodie. I turned to see Quinn watching and shaking his head.

"What the hell are you doing?" I could see the tension as his body vibrated with anger. He knew what I was planning, which meant he would have to stay with the children.

"I have to help them," I whispered. I sat on the side of the bed to put on my sneakers without looking up.

"Wow? How, in the hell, do you think you will be able to do that? You have no fucking energy, LaToya! You are running on fumes, and I will not see what happens when you are empty." I stood up, but he was right in front of me. I looked up, reaching for him and touching his chest. I closed my eyes and gathered every ounce of strength I possessed. I had to do this because the one who took them would die, but they had to know something was wrong. When I passed out, I saw what had happened, and that woman wasn't who she appeared to be. Garrett and Lily weren't the only ones who needed to be saved.

"I am twice marked, Quinn. It isn't that you share my power, but you hold what I can't in my body. I am your mate. You will restore me with what you have if I am low." I looked up and saw the pain in his eyes, but he knew I was right. I had to do this because he would do the same if it were reversed.

"Take it then," he gritted through clenched teeth. I stood on my toes and reached up, pulling his head down to my lips, and breathed deeply.

Michael

The building shook, but none of us moved. I was done with the bullshit and opened my mind to every vampire, searching through thoughts of the easiest ones. The screaming became louder, and I realized it was Joziah. I turned, heading for the door to see what the fuck was going on. I turned back, seeing the Blue Bloods that filled the hall on their knees, pulling themselves up. I caught my eyes with my mother and pointed to the room where Sara was being held.

"No one enters that fucking room," I growled. I looked at Douglas and Camila as they stood from the tearing I did to their minds.

"No one in this build will leave. Do you fucking understand me? She is here, and I want her found and brought to me." Before I could look away, my eyes went down, seeing my uncle on the floor. He was pushing himself up, but I could tell he was weak and in terrible pain.

"Go! Go, Michael. I will find her, my King." Next to me, he was the strongest of us all. That proved to me that his strength was nothing to look down on. I didn't know if he would survive if it were true about his Kindred Soul. His strength may not save him when I take her head. I didn't speak as I turned and disappeared outside. I looked around and the fallen people and screaming men, women, and supernaturals who just came to look. I saw Joziah holding a Hunter to his chest. His blade was sticking out of the man's back, and I saw the pain in his eyes. I looked over at a human woman in a torn skirt, broken heels, and a shirt that would barely close. I read over her thoughts, getting the last events as I took my tux jacket off to put it around her. She looked at me, still clutching a camera in one hand and her other touching a man lying against her leg.

"Thank you," she whispered, and I saw everything as she had. I walked through her mind, but I saw no one resembling Angelic. What I saw had me shaking my head. Someone always wanted more damned power and would hurt or kill whoever got in the damn way. I saw Joziah throw himself over the people he was protecting and send out a shield of protection around the hotel and whoever he could reach. Before he landed on top of the terrified people, I watched through her eyes as he threw the blade at the man with the bomb, and it hit just as the man clicked the button. I pulled back after everything for her went black putting two and two together until the katana found its home.

"Help should be arriving very soon. Please get your people to the steps of the hotel." I said, noticing she had just realized who I was. Her heart rate picked up as she licked her chapped lips. I saw a slightly shaking nod as she held the camera with a firmer grip, angling it to face me. I ignored it and moved to Joziah as Devana and her sister Dali pulled other humans and Hunters to their feet. Joziah went to his knees with the body as he removed the katana from his chest. I looked at the Hunter, seeing it was Beverly Ryder's son Zareh.

"Why?" Joziah asked, holding the Hunter as the life left his eyes.

"At least she won't be able to use me any longer. I never wanted...stop. Stop–" Blood oozed from his mouth, and I moved to try to help.

"No," Joziah said, stopping me. "Bring him back will put him back in the same state that made him do this." He seethed. He laid the man on his back when more shots broke out, and Hunters faced each other. Jamari Ryder stepped forward, looking around and spotting her brother dead.

"You see, Baltimore! They kill whoever they want and do nothing. They use bombs to scare you into compliance." I was about to knock this chick off her damn feet. I brought my hand up when Joziah caught it, shaking his head.

"There will be worse things coming now that the seal is broken. We need everyone meaning humans and supernaturals, on the same side. Do not give them any reason to doubt you are not what Taria has presented you two to be." His words hit home, and I understood, but I didn't fucking like it. They were playing a game with lives, and I did not have time for it. I had to find Angelic and get Lily, but instead, I am here playing God damn politics. Joziah stepped forward as the sirens of police cars and emergency services showed up.

"I will not argue with a Hunter who doesn't know the meaning or reason behind the name. The truth will always come out, and the people will judge and choose what side they will be on. It happened before you thought about it, and it will happen again. Now take your people and get the fuck out of here." His voice was level, but his fist glowed with a white power I have only seen one other person have. I watched as Jamari looked from Joziah to her brother before her, and her followers turned and disappeared into the night. That's when the police roared commands over a loudspeaker.

"Weapons down!" I didn't have time for the bullshit. I looked at Joziah, and he motioned for me to go. I could do nothing here, but I think his purpose was to get me to show my face. I was faster than anyone could see and returned to my hotel. With everything going on, Joziah never loses sight of the goal, of what he was out here to do. He was three steps ahead of the game, but I hoped he understood that if something happened to my children, whatever was coming won't be shit compared to the hell I would rain down on this world. I moved past the human clustered together on the steps of the hotel.

"Camila, I need you out here handling this shit while I find my daughter. Help all you can and cool down the situation, but let the Hunter take point." I spoke into her mind. I came through the doors just as she got to them. Fear in her eyes made me realize she couldn't answer my mind. Someone held every mind closed, and if I dug too hard, it could damage them in ways our healing couldn't fix.

"Go. I will handle this," I said, pushing her out the doors. I could feel her relief but also her anger and fear. Her father and sister were still in the building. I walked into the hall but knew no one would be there. I moved down the other hall heading for the grand ballroom. The doors slammed into the walls as I entered. Every Blue Blood that had arrived was present, including Angelic. No one moved as she held Lily to her chest with a silver blade to her throat. Sara stood tall, making sure no one came close as Angelic smiled.

"Now, once your Queen is dead and your children are, you will end up just like Gio," she spat. Everyone knew that when my grandmother went missing, and there was no way that she survived, Gio gave up, and nothing mattered, not his people or his child. Both sets of my fangs lengthened because she was right. Take my Kindred Soul, and children were effectively removing my heart.

"So, you really think you will get away with all this shit?" I growled. I hope she didn't think I would lie down and take this shit. She had the wrong mother fucking one. "Aight bitch. Let's do this," I hissed.

Chapter Twenty-One

TARIA

When I hit the ground, all I could see was dust falling down, and Hunters sprawled all over the ground, moaning. I turned to see my mother on her knees, breathing hard.

"I will be fine. Just a lot of power spent. This isn't our world, so we do not draw power from it. We are on our own with what we came with," she said, standing. She slowly shifted back into her normal form as the shield receded.

"It's all good. I have enough to take her ass out." I said, turning toward the temple. I could feel Garrett and knew he was still alive, but I didn't know how long that would last.

"There are panthers along the way. Push through and leave them to me. Get my grandson." No words needed to be spoken as we took off toward the temple. I held both blades in as I cut the plant and vines out of my way. The growls and claws that came at me were backhanded out of my way so my mother could handle them. I put on more speed, knowing I was getting close, as I brought my swords down on necks and panther paws that came at me. What I missed, I knew my mother had my back. I could see the steps of the temple in front of me. Four Druids stood before it with black balls of energy already waiting for me. "Shit!" I yelled as they sent their blast my way. I dodged the first blast and jumped as one hit a panther who almost had its jaws on my shoulder. I spun my blades fast as they continued to throw their black death toward me. The faster I moved my blades. The more intense the light became from the moon on the hilts. I looked down, seeing the crest on my shirt glowed as well.

"She isn't possible!" I heard the Druid's hiss when the light became so blinding my eyes hurt. A sudden blast of white energy pushed forward and hit the Druids, turning them all into dust. I ran up the stair before the ashes could hit the ground. I burst through the temple doors only to see a large black panther with red eyes. I could tell the panther had demon blood running through its veins, and I was sorry. My finger bled down my sword with a quick prick of my finger. I didn't have time to save this panther because Masika stood holding Garrett over a pit beyond him. The screams and hisses that came from the pit made my skin crawl. I knew if she dropped him, I would never see him again. That opening was a gateway to hell, making it clear how many demons could possess bodies. The seal was broken in more ways than one.

"Taria! Get Garrett. I will deal with him."

"I can take...."

"That is Femi!" She growled. I understood. Masika heard us, and she turned with a deranged smile. Her eyes bled, and her skin was turning sickly gray. She held Garrett with black claws that pierced his skin. Blood ran down his arms as he struggled to get free.

"A child for a child," she hissed and let him go.

"Garrett!"

Garrett

I could feel Taria close, and I knew she was coming. The warm feeling of the light that touched my arm felt like it was telling me to fight. I am a Cross, and I shouldn't be afraid. I had to help my mom and try to save myself. I looked down into the pit that burned and screamed. I could see hands, claws, legs, and everything you could imagine reaching out for me. I tried to turn my head when I heard the Taria enter the temple, but I knew she had to get through that enormous panther.

I could help him when Masika pours that dirty blood down his throat. I knew it was demon blood and what it would do to him. I whispered words Poppa taught me, praying that it would help him keep whatever mind he would have left. The screams became louder, making me look away from Taria. The light that came from her shirt made me less afraid. I looked back down, seeing demons clawing up with mouths open and deep red eyes that focused on me. They crawled over the sacrificed poor beings trying to get to me. I heard my grandmother and was so happy that Taria wasn't alone.

"A child for a child." Masika hissed to Taria, and I felt her claws slowly release me. I dropped, and right as I did, I pulled a small blade out and stabbed it into Masika's chest. She screamed as I fell. I didn't know what to do because I had one more blade left. Before the lead demon could touch me, hot heat covered me, and I rose. I was thrown to the ground next to the pit, and that's when I saw the portal. Aunt Toya stepped through with her arms held high and her eyes glowed blue-green.

"Garrett! Move!" I rolled out of the way as a clawed hand reached out, and everything around me burned.

Taria

I moved just as Garrett slammed his blade into Masika's chest. I wouldn't make it, and his screams tore at my heart. I tried using the burst of speed to get to him when Masika spun on her heel while pulling the blade from her chest, throwing it at my head. I moved, but she followed by striking out with those black claws. I leaned away but didn't see her other hand coming from the lower left side. Her black claws caught my leg, tearing open a wound as she danced back to not get my blood on her. Her red eyes blazed as she watched me fall to one knee. I used one blade to keep me from going down, and the other held out in case the bitch tried to attack.

I felt the air shimmer, and heat flowed over my back, making Masika move, and I saw Garrett being slammed to the side of the pit. I turned as the wind blew, giving my body time to heal.

"Garrett! Move!" It was Toya, and she made it just in time to save my baby. I pushed myself up as the Impundulu fought the poison from her claws, and my vampire blood healed the wound. I turned, seeing Masika fighting at the wind Toya was blowing out of her mouth, but

I knew it would end as she focused on the pit. The wind stopped, and Masika roared, making the temple shake to its foundation.

"He will die! You all will die, and nothing will stop the rise of Apu." She charged at me while her bones shifted in her body. I was up now and ready for the bullshit.

"Fuck, Apu!" I screamed as I met her. She was now a large tan panther with patches of missing fur. Her burning red eyes stared down at me, and it looked as if the demon tainted her; it distorted her panther form, making her into something else. I wasted no time and stuck out as a roar came from my left.

"Femi!" My mother screamed, and I saw the large black panther come for me, but she caught it by the paw and dragged him back. I stabbed in the same spot Garrett did because it was still healing. I knew the blades Garrett carried were tipped in silver and held the same point as mine. She twisted, but my blade still managed to cut her along the side. Her back paw snapped out, hitting me and making me slide across the floor. I slammed my blades into the hard stone and used the momentum to slow myself down and turn around. I pulled them free from the ground and sprung up, landing on her back. The beast roared, and the smell of rotting flesh and blood smelled of sulfur filled my nose. I reared back, taking both blades, and struck down her spine. She bucked, tossing me to the side, and I slid, hitting the temple wall.

"Mom!" Garrett yelled. I pushed up and looked toward his cries. He fought a demon that climbed from the pit. A few were coming for him while Toya focused on closing it. I had no idea how she knew how to close it, but it gave me an idea.

"Garrett, duck!" I yelled. I stood fast-moving as the lightning in my body exploded outward, blasting the demon close to Garrett. I watched as Garrett spun on his knees and pulled out a small blade. The smell of his blood hit the air, and he jumped, stabbing the demon that reached for me in the eye. I couldn't hear his words, but I felt the power. I didn't stop as I struck the other two demons and kicked them back into the pit. "Garrett is you—" I didn't get to finish as a flying kick hit came at me. I moved, but the black claw caught me across the chest.

"My son is dead because of you. You should have never been born! My love died because of your mother and father," she growled, striking out at me again. I fell into Garrett, and I pushed him away from this crazy bitch. I looked down, noticing that the shirt absorbed the claws, that I wasn't bleeding, and my heart wasn't ripped out. My sword still stuck out of her back as she came at me with her mouth open.

"Your own wrongdoings led you to this heartache, not me or my parents," I said as I ducked under her enraged swing. I moved back toward Toya while still holding my blade in front of me.

"You're just a child! You know nothing about my sacrifice!" Her jaw dislocated as her fangs grew longer. Her arms hung far past what was normal as she charged me.

"Toya?" I screamed. That's when I saw Garrett come out of nowhere and grab ahold of the blade still in her spine. He punches the hilt twice, making it go further in piercing her heart.

The loud roar had my mother and Toya turning and seeing Garrett being tossed to the ground hard. The punches he landed made the blade enter her heart along with the blood that coated it. She leaped at me, but I moved to the side, reached out, and grabbed the hilt, pulling my blade out, and kicked that bitch in the pit.

"It's almost done!" Toya cried as a demon grabbed her foot. I leaned over the edge, took my blade, and chopped off its hand. I watched it fall back into that burning hole as Toya pulled it closed.

"Maybe I should have yelled, 'This is Sparta' when I kicked her?" I said, looking at Toya. She smiled, but then collapsed. I caught her just before she hit the stone floor of the temple.

LaToya

I wanted to hug Taria, but I could feel the energy drain from my body. I lost my vision and could feel I was falling, but I was staring into that mirror again when I opened my eyes. "This magic comes at a price. Do you still wish to see it? It helps you save your family last time." The waspy voice bounced around in my mind. It was as if the mirror was showing a film that was paused.

"What is the exact cost?" I asked, looking at the woman standing in front of a mirror. She was dressing for what looked like a wedding or something.

"You use your power from within. If you use too much, you will die."

"Then I just have to know when to stop." I snapped. This woman didn't look the same as when she kidnapped Garrett. Something was different, and I knew I had to find out for Cam and Marcus's sake. The laughter was more creepier than the light touches I felt along my skin.

"If you say so, LaToya Aja Grey. No one knows until it's too late when they hit bottom."

"LaToya Aja Grey Savir," I said, stronger. "Show me," I said and waved my hand in the mirror, and it played.

I watched as the woman, Angelic, finished putting on a pair of earrings. She smiled into the mirror and spoke. "Jinx, this is it. I have my Kindred Soul and can finally escape this family." She smiled into the mirror. I watched as the mirror moved, and another woman or whatever it was spoken.

"Are you sure he is who you want? Why would you let him turn you into a vampire when you are a Witch of incredible power?" The thing hissed back.

"If I didn't know any better, I would think you weren't happy for me." Angelic frowned. "I can get out of here and still be close to Katherine. I will have everything I need. She turned away from the mirror, clearly irritated. She didn't notice when a hand and a foot stepped through the mirror and the scaly green-skinned woman stepped through. Her eyes glowed with a lime color, and behind her, I watched as a plant died. Angelic turned around. I guess sensing something was off.

"How... how did you get here? She asked, stepping back until her legs hit the bed. The woman walked toward a machete smile.

"You invited in long ago. It just wasn't time. Now is the time, says my master. You will now be in the prime position to remove the ones who will block his reign." Jinx moved like a snake as she grabbed Angelic. She opened her mouth wide just as a snake does to feed and swallowed her whole; it all happened so fast. The green lady's body split apart, revealing Angelic again coved in a sticky black substance. She shook as she fell back on the bed, screaming in pain as she clawed at her skin. I looked toward the door when I heard footsteps coming, and I was happy as shit someone was going to help her. A woman entered the room and closed the door rushing over to the bed.

"Angelic, Angelic!" I watched as Angelic's back arched up and slammed back down, and everything went silent and still. "Angelic!" The woman growled. She reached out, and suddenly, Angelic took a deep breath before sitting up. I couldn't do anything but watch as the woman touched her face, lifting it up to look into her eyes.

"how much time do I have?" Angelic asked.

"Did you have to make such a mess, Jinx?" The woman asked as she dropped her face. She turned for a closet, opened it, and reached into the back of it. Jinx pulled another dress out and held it up.

"Sara, how much time is left?" Jinx asked again as she stood. Sara spun around with a dress in hand.

"Enough time for you to get cleaned up and changed. Now let's get this plan in motion because Amu isn't going to wait forever." Sara sat the dress across the room and made for the door.

"Yes, mother," Jinx said with a sneer as Sara left the room. She turned and looked into the mirror, and I could see Angelic, the real Angelic staring out and screaming in her eyes. Jinx smiled in the mirror. "Don't worry so much, Angelic. I will take care of everything. Your family is following the wrong master, but that isn't my problem. Your own mother sold you out at birth, girl. Your body and soul always belonged to me." The mirror swirled, and all I could see was black.

Taria

I picked up her body and carried her over toward where Garrett landed. The temple was silent, but I could feel my mother's energy still near. I also could feel another who felt familiar to me, but I couldn't focus on that. Dropping to my knees, I laid Toya down and reached for Garrett.

"Garrett, Garrett?" I said, pulling him into my lap. His face was bloody, and I could see a bruise beginning to form. My fangs were already extended as I bit down into my hand. I made it deep, tearing away the flesh enough. It would take a minute to heal. I let my blood drip into his mouth and did the same for Toya. "Y'all got to get up. I... I can't–" I held Garrett close to my chest when Toya moaned.

"Why is your fat ass always putting blood in my mouth?" A startled laugh left my lips because I knew she would be ok. I don't know how long it's been since she said something like that, but it was a relief to hear.

"Aunt Toya, you told Lily and me that you and mom would not talk about each other like that if I can't call Lily a brat." Garrett coughed and leaned away from me. I was smiling, but the tears streamed down my face as I kissed him all over his face.

"Sorry, nephew, you're right."

"MOM!" I pulled back and realized we had no time for celebration because my baby girl was still fucking missing.

"Toya, we need to get back. That bitch Angelic took Lily and–" Toya pushed herself up, blinking fast.

"About that–" she said, telling a story no one else knew.

Chapter Twenty-Two

TARIA

Things were getting weirder and weirder by the damn moment.

"You got to be kidding? So this chick isn't even the real Angelic? Who the fuck is Jinx?" I said, getting to my feet. I heard a loud purring noise off to the side, and I saw my mother sitting next to what must be my uncle Femi.

"Yeah, and that shit was freaky as fuck. She ate her like a snake! I don't know what kind of Witch she is, but she deals with death. We need to get back like asap." Toya said, standing. She swayed, but Garrett put his arms around her. He was almost just as tall as she was.

"Yes, but how? You are damn near death's door. There is no way you can take us through the portal," I said, moving toward my mother. I had to return to Michael and find my baby before that snake-looking hoe did something to her. I didn't know much of anything about Angelic, but I knew we had to help her.

"Mom, is everything ok?" I asked as Garrett and Toya followed. My mother looked up with regret and pain in her eyes.

"I don't know. The only thing I could do was put the blood directly into his heart," she said, clutching the necklace. I always assumed that ruby or something.

"Dads?" I asked, looking at the panther.

"Your grandfathers," she said. She looked around me at Garrett and Toya.

"Oh, baby, I am so sorry," she cried, holding her arms open. Garrett went to her, and I turned to Toya.

"We need to figure out a way–" I started, but she cut me off with a shake of the head.

"I may not be able to return all of our asses, but I can get you and Garrett home."

"Naw, we can't leave you here! Are you crazy? Quinn would lose his shit if he knew what you are saying." I said, shaking my head no.

"I don't give two shits what either of you thinks. I know what I am doing, and with rest, I will be able to get Pearl, your uncle, and myself out of here. I am sure she can help me once Pearl regains her strength. Right, Mrs. Pearl?" Toya said, looking to the side of me.

"Yes, Toya." My mother said with a sigh. She didn't like the bullshit plan either, but what else could we do. I had to get back, and soon.

"Let's make this happen then. Garrett, stand next to me. I have a feeling time is going to be short." I looked back toward Toya as she swayed, mumbling words to herself.

"Envoyez-Les là où ils sont nécessaires. renvoyez-les à la Famille qui les aime." She spoke in hushed tones, and I realized she was speaking French. When the hell did she learn how to speak French? I roughly translated the words as "Send them back to the family that needs them. Send them to the family that loves them". I turned as I felt the portal's pull and pulled Garrett closer to my side.

"Hold on, Garrett," I said and picked him up, taking a running leap toward the closing portal.

Michael

Around me sat the Blue Blood council, and I also saw the human government officials there. I saw Luke standing there, holding them at gunpoint. He took a special interest in keeping the muscle at Agent Hood's head. Fear filled this room, but most vampires were more affronted about the situation. John Noble stood up, clearing his throat, getting Sara's and Angelic's attention. Regardless of who in this room thought at the moment, Lily was a princess in the Royal family. No one will make a move.

"Lady Sara, what the hell is the meaning of this? You need to control yourself, child," he said with disgust. Angelic laughed as she pulled Lily closer to her. Lily cried and tried to twist out of her grasp. I saw her skin ripple, and Angelic noticed as well.

"Don't you move. Turn into that little mutt again, and I will bite your tail off," she hissed at Lily.

"Hey! Don't fucking talk to her. Talk to me! Sara, you claimed to be doing all this because you wanted answers about your son. Well, there he is! What the hell else are you up to?" I tried focusing my mind against theirs but came up against a powerful barrier surrounding them.

"Daddy!" Lily cried when Angelic nails dug into her skin. I knew if I moved, she could kill her before I could break whatever spell she had going on. I could feel the evil and demonic presence but sensed no demons. That only meant they were receiving help from one.

"What the fuck do you want?" I growled, and I could feel my anger winning over my control. "You want the throne!" I saw greed flash in Sara's eyes as she looked at Angelic.

"You are damn right. I want the throne, but not this one."

"What!" Sara said, looking at her daughter in confusion. "What the fuck are you doing?" She growled at Angelic, who just lifted the side of her top lip to show fang. While they were talking, I worked on the shield they had protecting them. I looked around and saw some of the council moving into place to see if they had a better advantage.

"Oh, shut the fuck up, Sara. This was never about Van Allan and the ruling. That was set in motion to eliminate all Vaughns, and you still could manage that! Then you were told to kill off every Cross Hunter, and you failed in that as well. Now I am here to fix all that, you silly bitch."

"I gave you my child's life!" Sara screamed.

"What the fuck did you do?" The growl was from Caleb, who stood in shock at the play-by-play. Sara and Angelic both snapped their heads in his direction. Angelic moved forward a bit, still holding Lily close. One hand was over her throat, and the other restored her mouth.

"You think you have been with the poor sweet Angelic would have made it this far in the backstabbing of this council. Wouldn't she ever survive being turned if it wasn't for me?" She growled. Her eyes held a lime-green glow as she spoke.

"Who the fuck are you?" Caleb asked with deadly calm. She laughed as she stepped back, and I could see that Sara wasn't about to forgive and forget. Sara struck out, knocking Angelic off balance. I did what I could, but I moved to grab Lily, grabbing her and landing on the side while she was distracted. I turned, seeing my mother, and handed Lily to her.

"Get the fuck out of here," I yelled, turning back to the two idiots. I knew more was happening but would beat it out of both. I took a step when a loud gunshot went off. Everyone stopped and turned to see Luke holding the gun in the air.

"I will kill every last human before you can stop me." He turned to face his mother and stepsister. Kill her and be done with it. She isn't needed anymore." His voice held no emotion or inflection. I flicked my eyes to the right and saw Malia and her father move toward the boy. I looked to see if my mother had left the door when I saw two Druids appear behind her. I didn't know how the fuck they managed to get in, but I was going to find out. I just had to choose who would be saved and who would die.

"Luke, get over here and help me get rid of this bitch. She was never a true Van Allan in the first place." Sara spat. Her fangs were down to her chin, and she seethed at her daughter. "I never wanted a daughter, anyway. I hope she can still hear that, and our deal ends here." Sara said.

"Who said he was talking to you?" Angelic said as her hands shifted into green claws, and she cut Sara right down the middle. Screaming from the humans started as the Blue Bloods all moved.

"Now that I have all of you here simultaneously, shit should be easy." I wanted to release my power and take her ass out, but doing that would kill many close to us. Lily was still here, and my mother was as well. As the words set in, the council realized this was a setup. She raised her hands in the air looking into the ceiling and showing all of our reflections as a portal opening appeared.

I saw all this in the space of a second, and I had to choose who to save cause there was no way I could save everyone, not with what was coming through the portals. I turned back, flinging my arms out toward a Druid as I let a power blast slam into another's Druid chest. They went flying, but I saw the black balls of energy had been thrown. The balls of energy were heading for my mother's back. Caleb took down another Druid with swords I didn't know he had. I saw my mother throw a shield to protect her and Lily, but I knew it would get through. She was strong, but her powers had not fully returned. That's when a shimmer happened in front of them. A bolt of lightning came crashing into the room. My heart made one solid beat as Taria stepped through with my son.

Taria

Stepping through, I dropped Garrett and pushed him toward Katherine and Lily. I could feel the connection I had to the Earth and to Michael. I could tell I was running on fumes, but as I breathed, I could feel my power increase. "Michael?" I said, looking up at the clawed hands reaching down through whatever gateway the bitch Jinx created.

"Taria! We need to stop Angelic. I don't know what the fuck is wrong with her."

"That isn't she!" I screamed and went directly into the chaos she was creating. I pushed vamps and humans alike out of the way. I swore I saw Luke, but I wasn't sure because he slipped from sight. I slammed into her, knocking her connection to what looked like the pit Toya had just closed. "I know who you are!" I said, slamming her head into the marble floor. She screamed, hissing in my face as she pushed me off. She slithered back, and the lime green of her eyes shone from her face. I could see someone else behind those eyes, and I didn't want her to die along with this bitch.

"I see you, Jinx!" I said to hold both my twin blades. I had one knee on the ground, and my other leg stretched out, supporting me. I saw the flash of surprise in her eyes. "Yeah, I know what the fuck happened, and that shit ends tonight!" I said. I could feel Michael dealing with the open gate and see some demons slipping through. The Blue Bloods were holding their own, and they should be. This is what they are supposed to be doing, anyway. We were all here to stop what was happening right now. We were here to protect those who could not protect themselves.

"You know nothing!" Her voice sounded like it held so many souls that she stole. But all that shit stops here. I didn't want to kill Angelic, but to stop this madness, I would do what I had to.

"I know you and your master have been at this for a long time, but when I send your bitch ass back to him, give his ass a message." I could feel my fangs lengthen as I moved forward. I heard the breaking of glass as I held out my hand for the lightning that came to my call.

"Impundulu was defeated! You cannot wield...." She hissed as I slammed the bolt of lightning into her. I ducked under her clawed hands, slicing her stomach smoothly. She moved forward, using her fangs as she landed on my shoulder. She bit down hard, making me scream in pain.

"Mommy!" I heard Lily's voice, and I prayed she stayed away. I reached behind me, grabbed her, and flipped her over onto her back.

I watched as my blood burned her from the inside, and the pain filled her eyes. Dropping my swords, I leaned over her and touched her face. I pulled as if I were removing a demon. In a way, she was a demon, but worse. She was a Witch who turned dark and sold herself for demon-like power.

"NO! You can't do this! You're not supposed to be ab...." She screamed as I pulled, making the green fluid pour out of Angelic's mouth. It leaked from her ears and nose as I watched the bitch die.

"Mommy!"

"Lily, stay back!" I screamed. The oozing stopped, and Angelic lay still on the ground, eyes wide open. My blood would harm anything that wasn't demonic, and I pulled that out of her. "Angelic," I whispered. She didn't move, and I couldn't hear a heartbeat. I stood, lifting her up from the ground to lay her on a table that wasn't turned over. I looked back, seeing that Michael Had the portal under control, and I wondered how he could manage it. I turned back, looking at the woman trapped in her body for hundreds of years. "You have to fight! You have children wanting to know their real mother." I said, almost choking.

"Mommy!" I turned while reaching to the middle of my back for my short sword.

When I spun to see Lily, a green scaly woman held her by the throat.

"Anybody is better than none." She whispered as her mouth opened. I moved, and I saw Lily twist and shift. She turned in her grip and sank her teeth into Jinx's shoulder. She dropped the pup as I slammed my sword into her stomach. I twisted the blade and pushed it up. Holding the wound, I pulled it back out as she fell to the ground. I lifted my arm for more lightning and sent every strike into her body when it came. I watched her body split open, and her insides bubbled, but her heart still beat. I raised my sword again, but before I stabbed her heart, Lily darted forward, sinking her teeth into the heat and tearing it from the body.

"Lily!" I screamed, dropping to my knees to scoop her up. "Don't eat that," I said, but it was too late. She whimpered in my arms, and I stood to look for Garrett. He stood up, looking like his grandfather holding his blade. The demon at his feet sizzled and sank to the floor.

"Lily, mom!" She yelled, running to me. I saw Michael leaning over on his knees as the portal snapped shut. I looked around. The wounded were everywhere, but we were still alive. I grabbed Garrett and took them over to Michael, who reached out for Lily, me, and Garrett. I could feel his relief but also his anger. I leaned back, and he kissed my forehead before we all stood together. He kept Garrett close to his side as he stepped forward. There was moaning and talking and plenty of blame thrown around the room. I saw Caleb and Katherine hovering over Angelic's body. Michael looked around, and his eyes blazed gold. I could feel his power grow, and I could feel how out of control it was. I stepped forward, placing a hand on his back.

"Silence!" He growled. The building rumbled. All motion stopped as every gaze fell on us. Lily wiggled, and I put her down. She pushed up against Michael to help with his anger, but this was well deserved.

"None of you may have known about Angelic, but some of you bastards knew what Sara and her family were up to. If not you, then someone in your family was a part of it, and I will find out who they are and rip their hearts from their chest." They looked around at one another, and we all knew some were guilty and some just ignorant. "Shit changes today. You see what just happened here, and it will keep happening. You all were made to defend our people from shit like this. None of you have been doing the job!"

Chapter Twenty-Three

KATHERINE

I stood next to my brother as he looked over at his wife. I couldn't look into his eyes because I knew exactly what he felt. How could we not have known all these years that something wasn't right? After being married and changed, we thought the changing from human to vampire caused her different attitudes. She was sometimes more assertive and direct and didn't take shit from anyone. I thought it was ok initially, but I noticed how close she became with her mother and how more like a Van Allan she became. The gifts she possessed as a Witch were slim to none except for the gift of making grass grow and flowers bloom. I should have known when her gardens began to be neglected, and she left it up to the grounds for people to care for.

I thought I saw the old her when the children were born, at least for a while, but once they became independent, she returned to herself.

"How did we not see it?" Caleb asked. His voice was toneless at this moment as the pain tore through his body. I had to get word to the boys. They needed to be here for their father.

"She hides her deep, Caleb." He turned to me with dark eyes as his hair glowed. His pain rolled off him in waves, and I completely understood if he lashed out. He opened his mouth but slammed it shut when the ground shook. He hovered over Angelic, protecting her from whatever else was happening when power surrounded us all.

"Silence!" Michael growled, and the building rumbled. All motion stopped, and I turned to face my son. I saw a bloody Taria by his side, eyeing everyone carefully.

"None of you may have known about Angelic, but some of you bastards knew what Sara and her family were up to. If not you, then someone in your family was a part of it, and I will find out who they are and rip their hearts from their chest." Everyone looked around at one another, and we knew some were guilty. Also, we knew some were just ignorant. "Shit changes today. You see what just happened here, and it will keep happening. You all were made to defend our people from shit like this. None of you have been doing the job!" The power receded, and everyone breathed and released their clenched fist.

"We knew nothing of this plan here today! We came for the crowning and to discuss those pups. You let into our hierarchy." I looked to see who in their right mind would still bring this shit up after all this.

"What the fuck did you just say, Patrick?" Michaels's voice was deadly, and I knew it was time for the bullshit to end about my grandchildren.

"It's true! Who is to say an Alpha wolf couldn't claim rights to our throne if allowed?"

"Look around, Patrick Parks and everyone thinking along those lines. We have more to worry about than species bullshit!" I could see Michael holding back. I saw Nora move forward.

"Be that as it may, my King, I am the keeper of our laws, and it is written if a child is not a part of the Royal bloodline, they are not seen as such. You are right that they are your children but will never be given the same rights." Nora stated. She held her head high and gave Taria a dismissive look that I knew my daughter had caught.

"Be that as it may, Nora Augustine, my son is of my bloodline, which makes him Royal ever since of the word. I dare you to treat my children in any other way but with respect." Taria growled as Michael held her in place. Nora raised a brow, looking her over, and sniffed.

"Well, that must be proven and entered into our books." She said, flashing fang. Michael studied the woman until she noticed his stare, and she bowed her head.

"She is your Queen, my King, and if that is her blood, then so be it." She turned to fade back into the crowd, but Patrick raised his voice again.

"That may be a proven fact, but what about the other? I heard no claim of blood ties for her."

"She is my child!" Michael roared. Taria couldn't stop him this time as he lifted Patrick off the floor, pulling him close.

"My King... that... that may be so, but the law is the law. We enforce the laws set by Gio and that are backed by the crown." I could smell his fear, but he held fast to the knowledge he knew more about that law than Michael. I stepped forward, remembering what I found going through Lily's things.

"Michael put Patrick down; he is right. The crown backs the laws, so others are afraid to break them." I said as Michael turned his golden eyes in my direction. He let the idiot go, who didn't realize he marked himself for an investigation.

"See, your mother understands. She is the Queen, and us—" Before I could stop it, Michael was in his face again, both fangs at his neck. Patrick shook from fear as he leaned in submission.

"My mother was Queen, but your Queen, along with the rest of you stuck-up bitches name is Taria Cross, and that you will respect. I will say this only once: *she is your Queen, and you will never forget that.*" He pushed the fool away, making him stumble into another Blue Blood from his house, who pushed him away.

"As I was saying. Lily was part of a pack that held blood ties with my family for centuries. I had no idea that anyone from that pack was left, so she is, in some instances, part of our family." Mummers arose as Michael looked at me. "I never got the chance to say anything," I whispered to him.

"Wait, that may give her some rights, but she is not Royal. She does not carry any of your blood." Nora said, shaking her head. I felt a pulse of power and heard little feet on the floor.

"Lily!" I turned to see Garrett take his shirt off and put it over Lily's head. She turned and ran over to Michael, holding his hand.

"I am family. This is my daddy, and I am his princess." Lily smiled up at Nora and every other vampire in front of her. Nora still shook her head.

"Child, I am afraid you do not–"

"No! You don't understand. He is my daddy, and we are family." She said, looking around. She turned until she saw her pink teddy bear backpack and ran for it.

"We all need to get cleaned up and resume the crowning tomorrow. Also, we…"

"See… see the look, daddy." She held a small leather book out to Michael. He took it from her, frowning, and then looked at me. "This is my grandfather's journal, and it tells stories of him looking for a dragon who is my great-great-grandma, right? It tells me when he met my grandma and had to leave before my mommy was born. Her name was Rose, and that's why everyone calls me Lily because we have to have names like flowers." She turned to look at me, and I tried putting it all together, but it was impossible.

"Lily, my brother, never had any children," Michael said with a sad smile.

"Not the bad brother, daddy. I'm talking about your other brother, Jessiah. His name is Jessiah Vaughn, and he is my grandfather's, right grandma?" She turned to look at me, as did the older Blue Blood, who knew of Jessiah.

"Oh, my God," I cried, realizing the eyes were the same because she was part of my son and part of me.

"Too many secrets." I heard Taria say as tears filled my eyes.

Joziah

I could feel my daughter as she reentered this world, and I knew I had to do everything I could while she fought her battles. Camila helped smooth things with the police, and we started helping those get the emergency service people. The Hunters helped us move, and we used our healing when we could. If we didn't think that person would make the hospital trip, we healed as much as possible. Jamari ran off. But I knew things with her, and her mother wasn't over. I saw the woman I gave the camera to standing at an ambulance's doors. She watched as they loaded her cameraman on the stretcher and into the van.

"He will make it," I said, nodding. She looked at me and held her hand — Victoria Miles of Channel 4. If you ever need anything, please give me a call. She looked around, but her purse was long gone.

"I am sure I can find you if need be." I heard a whistle and reached out, pulling Victoria to the side. The knife flew by and embedded itself in the building's concrete behind us. I banged on the van's doors, and they took off. I pulled the woman down beside me as I looked for Beverly. I knew it was her; it would be no other.

"Stay down," I whispered and jumped to my feet.

"Always the hero, Joziah," Beverly said. I looked up, and she stood three floors above me, flanked by her daughter and other Hunters who followed her.

"How about you say that down here," I said, holding out my arms. All motion and noise stopped as if it were just us out here.

"This all could have been different. Now we must go to war," she said with a shake of her head.

"That's what you choose to do. You know the saying, Beverly. We, like Hunters, are here to protect everything that is to come."

"I am sorry, Joziah, but being on the other side will give me the best advantage."

"Even if it means killing your own Hunters. Killing your own son!" I pointed to the body lying on a pile of rubble. Her eyes shifted, and that's when I moved. I leaped into the air drawing out my knife, but she moved, pushing another Hunter in front of her. She danced back, pulling her daughter as other Hunter attacked. She jumped through a portal that formed on a wall as I fought to get to her. Knocking down each Hunter, the portal closed, and Hunters started leaping from the building to escape into the night. The last I saw was her smile, and I heard her parting words.

"Hunters will Reign!" She was gone.

Michael

I didn't want to leave Taria and the kids, but I had to put this shit to rest for the night. I knew things would be different once becoming King came into effect. I didn't want to believe all the backstabbing and secrets surrounding us would affect my small family. After Lily dropped that knowledge on us, I had no fucking idea what to say. I had another brother I knew nothing about, but it seemed as if the elder vamps in the group knew exactly who Lily spoke of. I watched my mother and uncle cry over Angelic's body. I knew there was nothing I could do, and that fucked me up inside.

"Baby, can we go home? Toya called and said my mother, and he made it back. Quinn is on the way to get her, and I want to see her before she goes." Taria said, holding Lily in her arms. I could tell it would be a minute before she let them go far. Shit was the same for me because I dragged her and the kids with me with every move I made.

"Yeah, I just need to take care of some things, and we can go. I will let Camila handle the rest." Lily lifted her head off of Taria to look over at my mother.

"Mommy, I want to go sit with grandma." I watched the war in her eyes as if she should. She kissed Lily and put her down.

"Garrett, go with your sister." He nodded and took her hand, and they went over to Katherine.

"We have so much more to do, and I can tell this added more to the pile."

"Yeah, but we got this shit, sweetheart. It's just the beginning, but we will bring it to an end." I said. We both turned at the loud gasp of air and saw Angelic rise from the table.

"Ahh, hell, naw!" Taria said, pulling out her blades.

"No, No, wait." Lily stared into her eyes for a moment and smiled. She turned and sat beside Garrett as Caleb fell to his knees. "I have no idea what our children are," I said seriously.

"I have no clue, but they are mine." She was right about that, and I pushed her to them.

"Let me handle this so we can go," I said, facing Camila and her father. It was time to clean out the Blue Bloods and get them on the path they should have never strayed from.

Chapter Twenty-Four

TARIA

I couldn't believe Beverly's punk ass got away after all that. This tells me that Apu has had a plan long in the making, and it is scaring me to think about what he's got coming next. I wanted to wash today off, but it was hard for me to leave Lily and Garrett for any amount of time. I knew Michael could feel the hesitation when I got them home and cleaned up. I was so pissed that Garrett had bruises and marks on his body. Lily had a few scratches, but I was worried about that heart she took a bite of. Michael assured me that she didn't really know what she was doing. Shifter children in their animal form tend to attack when threatened without thinking.

I got out of the shower and walked into the bedroom. I rubbed my stomach, still trying to figure out why I still felt nervous, I guess. It seemed to have settled since I had all my family back together and at least one threat neutralized. I could feel Michael when he came through the door, and I turned to face him. His eye roamed my body as I pulled out a large tee and pajama pants.

"Who is..."

"Shani is with Lily, and Garrett is with Cam," I said as he closed the doors.

"Cam is home? When did he get in?"

"A few minutes ago. We can't reach Marcus right now, but Cam says he will fill him in. Things will be strange for them, but I think shit will work out."

"Cam can handle it. He may have already suspected something was wrong. You know him and his feeling and shit." I said, walking over to him.

"Yeah, I still have questions about that. Hell, my mother has locked herself back in her fucking room. I can't believe I was never told about having another brother. It's bullshit. It's as if secrets run this world. How many more will it be until we know everything?" I pulled him down to hug him, and he kissed me. I hated that I couldn't feel him when I left to get Garrett, and it felt like my heart was ripped out.

"What about everything else? What about this whole crowning situation?"

"Oh, that shit is happening tomorrow, and I have to meet with the officials who witnessed the bullshit tonight. I don't think I have the patience for this King shit."

"Yes, you do. What about the Blue Bloods? Do you think they will give this crowning a hard way to go? I know some of them still don't approve of me."

"Fuck them and what they think. Camron is back because of his mother, but he will also find out who else was in on the plans. For now, we need to keep our guard up."

"I'm good with that, but what about the kids? I mean, my stomach is still flip-flopping around thinking about someone being able to take them off our land. I thought that was impossible," I said, pulling away. I sat on the bed, trying to figure out how it happened.

"First, when Toya and Pearl returned, she immediately started working on the holes in the warding. No one thought to ensure no one could use a portal going off the property because enemies could get in. That was my fault with that. I should have never given her access to our home," he said, sitting beside me.

"Naw, that's not on you. She was family, and how were you supposed to know what the hell that Witch demon had going on? I felt something off, and so did your mother. We should have thought it through better. This was all of our fault."

"Yeah, I feel you, but I am the King, and with all these powers, I should have been able to do something."

"HA! Ok, with all your powers that you can't fully explain or control. It's new, and you still need time to learn." I said, rubbing my stomach. Michael reached out, placing a hand over mine, and smiled.

"So, you mean to tell me you're still going to ignore the fact that you're pregnant?" I pushed his hand away because it was no way. With everything going on, we didn't have time for any of that.

"See you trippin'. We have no time for that, and I am a newly made Michael. My body isn't ready for something like that. I mean, that's what Lydia said, anyway." I shrugged.

"When did you talk to her about this?" He laughed and pulled me back down to the bed.

"I had personal women questions I refused to ask you about," I said with a side glance.

"Well, what she said is true, but with you, sweetheart, what has been normal? You are having my baby, whether you think so or not." He let my hand go and stood up.

"I need to check on my mother and get some answers. After the ceremony, we all need it to sit down and deal with our shit. I still can't believe I am raising a great-niece." He closed his eyes and shook his head.

"I told you there was a connection. I told you from the jump they belonged to us," I said, pulling him back down. I laid back, pulling him over me to look his face over.

"Yeah, you said some shit like that." His hands rubbed my sides as he moved us to the middle of the bed. I tried pushing the whole having a child out of my mind, but I knew he was right. He leaned in, licking my neck as he settled between my legs. "I need to go and handle some things, and we can pick this backup." I heard him talking, but I was lost. I was lost in the sensation of feeling him close to me and smelling his scent. I didn't know when the next time would be when we were attacked, and I refused to miss out on having him with me — having him close and inside me.

"Ok. You can in just a few minutes." I whispered. I felt my fangs descend, and I sank them into his neck. I felt him rubbing against my core and knew these few minutes might be a few hours.

So many more questions needed to be answered, but they would have to wait. I stood in the Lillian-Garrett Hotel, and it looked as if nothing fucking happened. I stood on the raised platform where the battle took place, and it was spotless. Michael stood beside me with Katherine, Garrett, and Lily on my left side. I was always a woman who loved to wear dresses and flats, but this was so outrageous I couldn't wait to take it off and put on some leggings and a tank top. When I saw the black sequined cutout-illusion evening gown by Tom Ford, I laughed. I knew Toya would lose it over the dress, but it had nowhere for my swords. It was sexy as hell, and I could say I was rocking the hell out of it.

I looked at the Blue Bloods and turned vampires that stood before us as Derrick spoke and read from a book that looked to be older than my mother.

"Today, we celebrate our new King and Queen. This has been in the making for so long that we have forgotten. When the rightful King has been given the power and crowned, we all shall benefit from his gifts." I looked at Michael, trying to figure out what he meant.

"I will have the power to create more Blue Bloods, and when Blue Bloods find their Kindred Soul, I will have that power to turn them into a Blue Blood as well." He explained in my mind.

"That's a good thing. We need more Blue Bloods to keep the balance and to populate, right?"

"Yes, it is a good thing, but I can tell you that some will not want that to happen. They like the status quo, but I am here to tell them shit will be changing. Now that Cam is here, we can find the ones who will try to stop our progress."

"I'm guessing we also must keep looking for the rest who want to kill me?"

"Damn right, and if I didn't say it earlier, you look sexy as hell in that dress."

"This old thing Camila made me put on and pointed out they normally don't make dresses like this in my size?"

"Is that why her arm was broken when she left, and she was limping?"

"It was just a sparring match. Don't worry too much about it. She's fine," I said, shrugging.

"Well, once this is done, I am going to—"

"May I have the crowns, please," Derrick called out. Camron came walking up, holding two crowns. They were beautiful and simple. Nothing over the top because I didn't have it. It really didn't matter because I wasn't wearing the thing unless we had to attend something formal. I saw the smile but could see in Camron's dark eyes the pain that was there. I knew all this was an adjustment for him, and it was hard on him by Hayley not coming back just yet. His eyes lit up, though, when he stood before me. Katherine tapped my leg, and I leaned forward for him to place it on my head just as Michael did.

"Lookin' good, sis," he smiled, and Michael glared at him. He moved back, and Michael took my hand and stepped forward. After closing the book, Derrick turned to the crowd and lifted his hands toward us.

"King Michael and our new Queen Taria Cross - Vaughn." I side-eyed Michael, who didn't even give me the time of day as he raised our clasped hands. The cheers and claps filled the room as I saw my friends and family all smiling. At first, it would just be the Blue Bloods and us, but I refused this time. I wanted my family and friends here with us to show that we are not alone, and whatever plan some of these Blue Bloods may try will be slapped down every time because I knew who had my back, and now, they do as well.

As Michael dropped our hands, he held out one to quiet everyone.

"I want to thank everyone for doing their part here today. I also want it to be known that things are about to change, and if you don't like it, that isn't my problem. We have more important things to do than worrying about what species has the most power. We are all here to work together with one common goal. Stop the evil that is coming to this world because it doesn't matter who or what you are; they are coming for us all. On a happier note, I want to announce that we, Taria and I, are expecting." More cheers than I thought went up, and I smiled, slightly relieved. I heard Garrett say about time, but I would get him later.

I looked over at my mother and father, expecting them to be happy, but what I saw had me frowning. Their heads were together, and they weren't speaking with their mouths but mind to mind. My father caught my gaze and started forward when things went silent. I turned as a tall, well-built man with the strangest colored eyes appeared out of nowhere in front of us. His eyes seemed to be about every color in the rainbow and had me and others catching our breath. He was sexy as hell, but the look on his face was severe. I could feel Michael tense at my side, but he didn't move. However, Derrick and Cam were on it, but he spoke before they could confront him.

"I am also a King in this world. I have come to lay claim to what was promised to me. What I claim is the child of Taria and Michael. I will have what was promised to me and return when the time is right." My mouth fell open, and I felt Lily come to my side. I saw as this strange man's eyes traveled my body to land on my stomach and flicked to Lily. He turned his gaze back to me and nodded. Everyone, including me, moved, but it was too late, and he was gone just as quickly as he came. I turned to my parents, knowing this was another secret, but it was too far this time.

"You got to be kidding me!"

Epilogue

TARIA

One Week later

I sat at the table with my mother, father, and Michael. I should have never agreed to this interview with people I didn't know. This time at least, we met in an undisclosed location, and I kind of got over my aversion to reading minds. I just did the surface thoughts because I didn't want another agent sneaking up in this interview. I watched as the camera crew and reporter got their shit together. The woman who thanked my father about seventy times already finally sat down. She had a crush on Pops, but I said nothing about it.

I looked at my mother, but she had a pleasant smile. I could tell by the way she pointedly held my father's hand. She sent a message. I also heard her heart skip a few beats when looking at Michael. He sat in a chair that was scooted away from the table with massive arms over his chest. His low cut was fresh, and his goatee was neatly trimmed. I tried to get him to wear a suit or something to look as a King should, but he gave me the finger and put on his dark blue jeans, some designer white tee shirt, and a pair of red-bottom sneakers. I only knew this because Toya took it upon herself to fill everyone's closet. I looked back at the reporter, who looked at me and then at my mother and back before clearing her throat.

"Well, thank you all for coming. I want to say, as a victim of that night, thank you for everything you did." She said, looking at each of us. We nodded, and that's when my mother stood up. She moved to the back to stand with Derrick and Cam, not wanting to be on TV. I got it because I didn't want to either. I also knew she was still exhausted from dealing with my uncle, but that was another story altogether.

"No need for thanks, Victoria. That is what we do," Michael said with a half-smile. I saw her bite her lip while looking into his eyes. I fully understood the pull because it still happens to me, and I sleep with his sexy ass. She shook her head and turned back to my father and me.

"Well, thank you for doing this interview. Our viewers have had questions since the video's release that night," she said while swiping at her tablet.

"That is why we are here. We have no problems or are afraid to answer questions to the best of our ability." I said, leaning away from the table. I could hear the camera zoom in, focusing on us.

"Let's get started, shall we."

"Let's do it," I smiled.

"Well, when we first learned of all of you, we saw some creatures. Will they come back as well?" She kept an eye connected with me, so I guess I answered.

"Those creatures, Victoria, have always been around. They have never left, but we are doing what we can to ensure everyone stays safe. When we do find them, we take care of the problem.

"Some government officials say you caused this problem in the first place."

"They want to place blame because they do not know how to deal with it. We have offered our help to them." I shrugged. Michael leaned forward, catching her eye.

"Yes, do you have something to say on that?"

"I have reached out to officials in our fine government. We have repeatedly offered assistance, and now we are being taken seriously. It's a work in progress," Michael said, leaning away again. Victoria stared at him for a moment longer before looking at my father.

"Joziah, you saved Oliver and me, but why were those people or Hunters wearing what you claim as your symbol? They screamed the Cross's name. Some believe you staged it all. What do you say to that?

"Well, Victoria, you were there, and I am sure the video evidence proves itself. They had on something that was close to my symbol, as you put it, but it was fake. What does everyone say now, "Fake News?" It was to get this reaction in some people. People are already afraid of what's in the world and have no idea who to trust. This is what those people thrive on. All they wanted was chaos and to spread misinformation. They make people turn to the side that is here to help them.

Even if someone doesn't believe I am on the right side, I will save that person because we are here to do this. There is no more time for fighting each other over silly things. We all need to band together. Every species or race needs to start helping and saving each other." She nodded her head as she took in the answer given. She looked back up, catching my gaze again, and swiped on her tablet.

"Taria, tell us what do we do if those people—"

"Hunters," I stated.

"Yes, Hunters, come back, and who will defend us? You and your father are Hunters yourselves. What makes you any different from those who attacked us? You are a Hunter and a vampire, so why should we trust you?" I licked my lips and leaned forward into the camera.

"You can trust me because every time something happened, I was there to stop it. My team tries to make sure we protect any and everyone that we can. This isn't a game. If you don't think you can trust me because of what I am, that is your problem. My actions in each situation were to protect those around me. You may need your eyes checked if you can't see that from the footage. As for being a vampire, the only ones who should be afraid are the ones harming others and the creatures that come out to hurt or kill. They are the only things that should fear me." I growled as I leaned away, lifting a shoulder. "I mean, I have children. How bad can I be," I said, smiling. I noticed that Victoria had leaned away but laughed when I mentioned kids.

"Yes, you do, but that response was intense."

"It was truthful," I said, waving a hand and smiling again. I could smell the fear and tension and tried to lighten the mood.

"Well, a few more questions, and we will let you go. I know you all are very busy."

"It's no problem. Ask away," I said.

"If a human or supernatural were to spot any problems dealing with anything of supernatural nature, who should we contact?" She asked. I looked at Michael on that one, and his honey eyes glowed slightly as he leaned forward. His elbow went to his knee while his finger traced his lip.

"I would tell anyone to report it to their local authorities. We have been working on setting up protocols with the state and government agencies for such a thing. I would say do not approach or try to be a hero. Just call it in and let someone take care of it."

"Ok, that sounds like a plan. People will get behind." Victoria nodded as she looked at her tablet again.

"Our viewers asked my last question a lot, and I would also like to know," I nodded for her to keep going.

"Do your people have things under control, or should we start preparing for a supernatural war?" The question was good, but there was no way to answer it.

"I am a Hunter, and my goal is to fight what is evil and to protect every being on this Earth. Other Hunters and I are here to protect humans from supernatural events. There is a war coming, but people do not understand that it isn't the supernatural species that live among you which are the most dangerous. It's the ones you can't prepare for. That is why we are here, and if you want to fight in this war, all we need is support, not opposition."

"So the woman that attacked Joziah was right. Hunters will reign over us all?" I stared into my eyes, looking for a true answer.

"The woman you saw is a Hunter who is lost to us. She isn't on the right path and will be dealt with. Yes, Hunters Reign, but where she got it wrong is what we reign over. Hunter Reign over the ones who think they can take this Earth and hurt its people. We reign because no one would keep the evil in check without us but a Hunter. So for those who believe I don't have my proprieties straight, know this, I am The Vampire Queen, and I am a Hunter. To me, that is one and the same. I am here with the rest of my family to make sure evil does not take this world, and if a Hunter must reign over evil, then I am here to do it." I didn't notice my eyes were glowing or that I stood looking into the camera. Michael was beside me with a hand on my shoulder, and my father stood. Victoria looked at us all before turning to see the camera as well.

"There you have it, and I believe them. They are not here to rule us but to help everyone on this Earth. With strong words like that, why wouldn't you believe them? I will leave that question there, and I hope you will tune in next time. Thank you, and goodnight." I turned to look at Michael before we moved to leave. A short, stocky man that was helping the crew came over. He was pale as hell, with dark circles under his eyes. He looked at us before he came closer. He looked at Michael and then focused on me. I knew why because Michael always had this stay the fuck away from me look going on. I stepped forward and looked at the man until he spoke.

"I know you said to call the authorities, but can you help me?" He looked up into my eye, determined now as he stood straighter. "You said that you are here for us, so–"

"Tell me what I can do to help?" I asked, looking at him with concern.

"It's… it's my daughter. She hasn't been the same lately. I caught her washing the blood off her hands and face. She smells awful, and her room, I swear, smells of sulfur. I don't–"

"Get your things and take us to her," I said. The man turned and rushed away. I turned to my father, and his look told me everything. "Dad?"

"You know that the seal has been broken. From what you and your mother have told me about the pit, it's happening."

"What is happening?" I asked as Michael stepped closer. I leaned into his chest, taking in his calm demeanor.

"When the seal is broken, things are let loose, and greater things slip through. It seems we have another greater demon on our hands, and he is collecting." My eyes widened because I remembered what Donavon used those souls for. He gave them to a more powerful being than he was.

"You think it's Apu?"

"I think it's worse. Have you ever heard the stories about the old ones?"

"HP love craft? Yeah, of course, I laughed.

"Yeah, well, he may have gotten some names wrong, but he wasn't lying." That was it, and I was done because I would be damned if I fought something with tentacles, which was older than the world itself.

The End until next time...

About Author

E. Bowser is an author of paranormal romance, Fantasy, and Horror Fiction. She writes whatever stories her imagination can conceive. E. Bowser has always wanted to write a story that people would like to read and would fall in love with the characters. she loves when readers give their feedback so she can make her next book better. E. Bowser loves to read herself and takes great pleasure in doing so whenever she has the chance. E. Bowser started writing short stories about life, anything horror or paranormal when she was in middle school and still has not stopped. E. Bowser has been an independent self-published author since 2015 and has no plans to continue as long as her characters keep talking.

Thank you for reading. I hope you enjoy the series so far! Please review I love them or feel free to contact me on Facebook, Twitter, Instagram, good reads, book bub, or through my website. Thank you again for reading, and keep looking for more Deadly Secrets series!

Follow or contact me at the links below to see what is coming up next!

www.ebowserbooks.com

www.facebook.com/authorE.Bowser

https://www.bookbub.com/authors/e-bowser

https://www.goodreads.com/ebowser
Twitter: @ebowser0110
IG: @e.bowserbooks
TikTok: @ebowserauthor

Also By The Author

Deadly Secrets Brothers That Bite Books 1-5 The Deadly Secrets is an exciting series focused on Taria, Michael Quinn, and LaToya are friends and lovers fighting against evil forces.

Deadly Secrets Awakening Book 1

Deadly Secrets Revealed Book 2

Deadly Secrets Consequences Book 3

Deadly Secrets Consequences Book 4

Deadly Secrets Royalty Book 5

Deadly Secrets Novellas/Novelettes

This collection of stories will give you a glimpse into the lives of Taria, Michael, LaToya, and Quinn, along with many others. Sit back and fall back into the paranormal world of Deadly Secrets.

Desires of the Harvest Moon

Twice Marked Witches and Wolves

Rise of the Phoenix

A Vampire and His Alpha Mate
A Hunter Touched My Soul
Brothers That Bite Chronicles Volume 1
Trick Or Treat The Babysitters From Hell: Deadly Secrets Halloween
Rescued By Fire: Gio & Selena's Story
Scorched By Desire: Sire & Lydia's Story
Trick Or Treat A Night From Hell: Deadly Secrets Halloween

The Crown Series Books 1-3 On-Going series
This series would be best read if you start with Deadly Secrets Series Brothers That Bite books 1-5 and other novellas.

Taria, LaToya, Michael, and Quinn are back together again in Deadly Secrets Hunters Regin: The Crown Series. Taria Cross was turned into a Vampire by Michael Vaughn, and she became his Queen. Not only does she have to figure out this new part of her life, but she is a Hunter as well, and that is a whole other list of duties.

Deadly Secrets Hunters Reign Book 1
Their Sirenian Queen Deadly Secrets Story
Deadly Secrets A Vampires Temptation Book 2
Deadly Secrets When Queens Are Crowned Book 3
Twice Marked A True Alpha And His Witch Deadly Secrets Story

The Rayne Pack Series On-Going
Follow the Rayne Brothers as they find their Mates and fight the forces of evil. See how Dax, Max, Malic, Alex, Jarod, and Thomas fight for those they love while being attacked on all sides.

An Alpha's Claim Book 1
Submission To An Alpha Book 2

Dream Walker: Visions of the Dead On-Going Series.
What if you had the ability to see things before, they happened? Saw a zombie outbreak unfold before your very eyes? Could you embrace visions of the dead coming back to life? For Kaylee, who has been chosen to receive this gift, these visions are the beginning of a nightmare.

Dream Walker: Visions of the Dead Book 1
Dream Walker: Visions of the Dead Book 2
Dream Walker: Visions of the Dead Book 3
Dream Walker: Visions of the Dead Novella (Collection of short stories)

Made in the USA
Middletown, DE
09 June 2023